A TWIST OF FATE

This is a work of fiction. Names, characters, businesses, places, events, locales, and incidents are either the products of the author's imagination or used in a fictitious manner. Any resemblance to actual persons, living or dead, or actual events is purely coincidental.

A TWIST OF FATE

TRUE MATES GENERATIONS BOOK 1

ALICIA MONTGOMERY

CHAPTER ONE

"Yo! Girly, you're late."

Astrid Jonasson stopped in her tracks and cringed. She pivoted on her heel and faced her boss. "Yeah, sorry about that, Mr. G! The L-train's running late again."

Vito Garavaggio took a drag of his cigar and blew out a puff of smoke, then took it out of his mouth and pointed it at Astrid. "That's the third time this week. Why don't ya leave earlier? You know that train's always late, especially in this weather."

"I just ... forgot." She breathed through her mouth, trying not to inhale the acrid haze Mr. G's Cuban was creating in the tiny hallway. "I will next time."

"I swear to God, girly, they could invent a machine that can transport you from one place to another like in those TV shows, you'd still be late."

She tried not to let the irony of her boss' words faze her. "I won't do it again, Mr. G."

"See that you don't." He placed his meaty hands on his fat belly before turning around and waddling away.

With her enhanced Lycan hearing, Astrid could clearly hear him muttering under his breath about *if I didn't need her* and *if the girls didn't like her so much.* She let out a relieved sigh and sprinted down the hallway.

"Hey, Astrid," Coco greeted her as she entered the girls' dressing room. "Mr. G got on your case again for being late?"

"Yeah," she said as she shut the door behind her. "But, don't you worry. I took care of him."

Coco chuckled. "You know he's a softie. Unlike other places I've worked at before, he actually cares about us. Now," she stood up, carefully balancing herself on the sky-high heels on her feet. "Would you be a dear and take care of my top in the back there? That knot you do makes it easier to pull off."

"Sure, Coco." Astrid pushed the long, lustrous locks of dark hair aside and tied Coco's bikini strings into a slip knot. "There ya go."

"Thanks, babe. You're the best!" Coco gave her a kiss on the cheek before sauntering out of the door.

"Good luck out there!"

If someone had told her that she'd someday be using her knowledge from doing a year of Girl Scouts helping strippers get dressed—and undressed—she would have laughed at them. But then again, with the way her life had turned out the last couple of years, she wasn't surprised she ended up as a security guard at The Vixen Den, New York's premiere gentleman's club. Before this, she'd been a barista, dock worker, waitress at a Michelin star restaurant, bookstore clerk, and nanny, all before her grand old age of twenty-six.

Still, she considered this the best job she'd ever had. She could use her *unique talents*, and she loved her coworkers. Of course, it was also the best job she could never ever tell her family about, but that's why she had last told her mother that she was "working security during night shifts." Which, to her credit, was *entirely true*. She just didn't tell them *where* exactly.

Not that her parents or brothers were judgmental about these things, but a strip club—er, gentleman's club— wasn't exactly the most reputable of places to work, even if she was just hired on to protect the girls. She wasn't judgmental of the girls' jobs either, but personally, she drew a hard line at taking her clothes off to make a living.

As she crossed the room, all the girls greeted her happily. The Vixens—as they were called—loved the fact that she was a woman, which was one of the reasons she'd been hired. The previous bodyguard Mr. G had hired was apparently some mouth-breathing idiot who took his job way too seriously—as in, guarding the bodies of the women with his eyes. She had answered the help wanted ad because she'd been desperate to get out of that wait-ressing job, and she didn't care where she would go next, as long as she never had to serve Upper Eastside bitches who had to special order everything and tipped horribly again.

Mr. G had eyed her suspiciously when she came in for the interview. "You're certainly tall enough to be a body-guard," he said, "but can you protect my girls?" She proceeded to show him just how she could do it by putting one of his burly bouncers into a headlock, and she was hired on the spot. She knew her training would come in handy someday, and she did learn from the best.

"Astrid!" Fantasy, a tall, Amazonian-like girl with corn-rows hopped over to her, her perky tits covered strategi-cally by two glittering star-shaped nipple pasties. "I've missed you, girl!" She embraced Astrid, engulfing her in a flurry of feathers, Swarovski crystals, and a cloud of flowery perfume.

"How was the Bahamas?" Astrid asked.

"Amazing!" One of Fantasy's regular clients had flown her down to the Bahamas for the holidays. "Oh my God, I have so much to tell you. But first," she turned around and grabbed a gift bag that was sitting on her dressing table. "I got this for you. Merry Christmas!"

"For me? You shouldn't have." She accepted the bag and opened it. "Um, really, you shouldn't have." She took out the fabric gingerly and held it up. It was a dress—long and flowery, with sexy straps that showed off the back.

Fantasy crossed her arms over her boobs. "Girl," she began. "This dress would look fabulous on you. With your height, that skin, those tits." To emphasize, she poked Astrid in the chest.

Astrid groaned inwardly. Fantasy and some of the other girls at the club were always trying to give her a makeover. They kept telling her she was gorgeous and that if she wanted to, she could probably make a killing on tips if she ever wanted to get on stage. She thanked them gracefully, but continued declining their offers.

"Why do you keep hiding that bod under those clothes." Fantasy *tsked* and shook her head.

Astrid frowned and looked down at her faded jeans and T-shirt. "What's wrong with my clothes?"

"What's wrong? Those mom jeans don't exactly flatter your ass. And that shirt!" She pointed to the logo over the left side of her chest. "That company went out of business twenty years ago."

"I got it at the thrift store," she said defensively. "I like my clothes, okay? They're comfortable, and they let me do my job." She looked over at the table next to Fantasy's. "Hey, where's Petal?"

Fantasy swung her head around. "Hmm ... I'm not sure. I just got off the stage and I swore she was here."

A pit formed in the bottom of Astrid's stomach. "I should go check on her."

She asked a couple of the girls if they had seen Petal since the last set, but none of them could tell her where she was. She had shown up for her shift, but with the flurry of activity backstage and in the dressing rooms, no one noticed where she'd gone.

The pit in her stomach grew heavier. Petal had texted her this afternoon, saying she saw her old "boyfriend"—i.e., pimp—Leon, hanging around outside her apartment again. Astrid didn't see the text until she was on her way to work, and though she texted back, she hadn't heard from her.

Astrid had never met Leon, but according to Petal's stories, he was a piece of shit. He was mad when Petal broke up with him, and furious when she started dancing at The Vixen Den and made more money than she ever did working for him.

Apparently, the asshole had been trying to intimidate her, and even showed up at the club one day. A couple of the bouncers were able to scare him away, but Mr. G told them all to keep an eye out for him; Leon was violent and didn't take no for an answer. That was the only time Astrid had truly seen Mr. G look even remotely scared.

She searched almost every inch of the backstage and still there was no sign of Petal. As she walked back to the dressing room, she stopped and closed her eyes. *Concentrate.* She called on her inner wolf's abilities, opening up her senses so she could try and sniff out Petal's perfume from the various scents in the air. *There*, her wolf seemed to say. A faint trace of the brand she favored. She followed it, down the hall and toward the rear entrance to the alley where the girls would sometimes take their smoke breaks. When her ears picked up the sound of men laughing, and someone else sobbing, she froze.

Petal.

Dread formed in her chest, but was quickly replaced with adrenaline as her she-wolf pushed her toward the source of the sound. The wails grew louder and made the hairs on the back of her neck raise. She burst through the rear door, barely containing her superhuman strength as it flew open and slammed against the brick wall.

"What the fuck?"

The alley was well-lit, so she saw the three men clearly as they turned to her. The sound of a sob drew her attention, and she immediately noticed the small figure huddled in the corner.

"Petal!" she screamed, and sprinted over to where her friend lay in a heap on the dirty, snowy ground. "No. No!" She lifted her head up, brushing her hair aside. Blood flowed down from a gash on her eye and her lips were split. Tears flowed down her bruised and battered cheeks.

"A-a-astr—"

"Shh ... don't talk." Rage began to boil in her veins. Her she-wolf too, was furious; Petal was one of theirs, to protect and keep.

Slowly, Astrid got to her feet, hands fisted at her sides. "You motherfuckers," she said, turning around. "You all are gonna pay."

The tallest and largest of them laughed. "And who's gonna make us? You, little girl?"

The goon beside him licked his lips. "My man Leon over here," he gestured to the third man, "said we could have a taste of his sweet Petal once he was done with her. You gonna join us too?"

"Enough," Leon said, then spat on the ground. "This ain't your business. I'm taking Petal with me and that's final. Run along now and go back to your daddy on the Upper East Side."

"Ha! I'm from Brooklyn, you motherfucking asshole." Okay, so technically, she lived in gentrified Williamsburg and she was raised in Tribeca. "You're not going to get away with this!"

"Jamal," Leon barked. "Make sure she doesn't get away and go blabbing to the cops."

As the smaller of the men approached her, Astrid gritted her teeth. "I'm not trying to get away. And like I said," she cracked her knuckles together, "you guys are going to pay."

Jamal lunged at her, but Astrid easily ducked and lunged away. "Bitch, hold still!" he shouted. When he attempted to grab her again, she caught his wrists. "What the fuck? How are you so strong—ooowww!" He let out a string of curses as she twisted him around and forced him to his knees, bending his elbow into an unnatural position. "Fuck! Get this crazy chick off me!"

"For fuck's sake!" Leon cried. "Monroe, give that bitch ass a hand!"

Monroe ambled toward her and Astrid acted on instinct. She knocked Jamal out with a fist to the side of his head, then grabbed the small vial she kept in the pocket of her jeans and threw it at the lumbering giant. A cloud of green smoke materialized in his face, and his eyes rolled to the back of his head before he landed on the ground with a heavy thud. *Thank you, Dad and your cabinet of potions.*

"What the hell did you do?" Leon's voice was cold as ice. "Bitch! You're going down."

The sound of the gun cocking echoed through the alley. A split second passed before the loud explosion went off and once again, her instincts kicked in. She closed her eyes, and with a soft *poof* sound, she was behind Leon.

"What the—where?" Leon turned around, the gun in his hand still smoking from the shot he fired. "How the hell did you get there?"

By being a badass, motherfucking half-witch with the power to teleport. But she never got a chance to say it as her wolf ripped out of her skin. Leon had raised the gun to fire at her again, but her wolf sensed it and took over their body.

Astrid's wolf was pure white with red eyes—a rare albino wolf. It was huge, twice the size of a normal wolf, but that was typical of Lycan shifters like her. The she-wolf landed on top of Leon, pinning him down, growling and gnashing its sharp teeth at the terrified man.

"Get off! Get off me!"

The smell of urine made Astrid gag. *Coward.* Her she-wolf wanted to rip his throat out for what he did to Petal. *Make him pay,* it seemed to roar.

"What the fuck?" A gasp and several shrieks made the she-wolf turn its enormous head. *Shit.*

Mr. G and several of the girls were standing in the doorway, their eyes wide with fright and shock as they stared at the wolf. *Mother—*

And of course, the stupid wolf chose that moment to

withdraw, leaving Astrid in charge of their now-human body.

"Jesus H. Christ! Is that—Astrid?" Mr. G's normal ruddy face went completely white.

"I ... I ... can explain," she gasped and rolled off Leon. "Can someone please ..." She looked down at her naked state.

"I got you, honey." Fantasy sashayed over to her and took off the red fur-trimmed peignoir she was wearing over her negligee, then helped her put it on. She shivered visibly and rubbed her arms. "You okay? Jesus, how are you not freezing your ass off? You're like a heater!"

The snow had stopped some time ago, but the temperatures had remained below zero. As a Lycan, Astrid could adjust her body's temperature to suit the environment.

"Must be my Scandinavian blood. I—Petal!" She darted toward the girl, suddenly remembering her friend. "Petal, what—"

Petal screamed. "What are you? Stay away from me." Her body shook, and her one good eye was wide as a saucer. "Someone, help, please!"

Astrid's heart fell. "Petal, no, please—"

"Baby, it's okay," Coco soothed as she rushed over. "Oh dear. They did a number on you. It's okay, it's okay. Astrid, honey, you should ... maybe just give her some distance, okay?"

She nodded numbly and got to her feet. This was that bastard's fault. *Leon!*

Mr. G was standing over Leon, a booted foot to the

man's chest and the discarded gun pointed at his face. "Don't even think about it," he warned the man. "Someone, call 911."

"No!" Astrid pleaded. "Please, no police!" Oh God, her secret would come out. Not just hers, but her entire clan. Her entire *kind*. Humans were not supposed to know about Lycans or witches. She was going to be in big trouble, as she happened to be *both*.

"But we have to get help," Coco said. "For Petal."

Astrid swallowed hard as she looked over at her friend. They were right; Petal needed medical attention now, and these guys had to get locked up. "I can get help," she said, feeling the dread creep up in her.

"You got people to call?" Mr. G asked, raising a brow at her skeptically.

"Unfortunately, yes."

CHAPTER TWO

Zachary Vrost stared out the window of the penthouse apartment, watching as snow drifted down. The Hudson River was half-frozen, the ice glittering from the glowing lights of Manhattan's skyline.

While he missed the views from his London flat, this was *home*. He knew it. Every time he came home since he'd moved away, he felt New York's pull grow stronger. Even his inner wolf, the animal inside every one of his kind, knew it. Which was probably one of the reasons he chose to stay away. It made his wolf unhappy, but it wasn't the one in charge of their body.

"Tell me you've got a solution to our little political problem across the pond," a familiar voice said, interrupting his thoughts.

Zac folded his arms over his chest and turned around. "I know you think I'm brilliant when it comes to business, but I'm afraid even I can't help what's happening over there. Rest assured, we're putting things in place for any eventuality."

"I know you are," Lucas Anderson, one of his oldest friends, answered. "You're always one step ahead of everyone." He held two whiskey glasses in his hand and offered one to Zac.

"Well, as Chief Operating Officer of Fenrir Corporation's London office, it *is* my job to be one step ahead." Zac accepted the glass. "And soon, I guess, I'll be reporting to you?"

"Ah, he told you?" Lucas' face was inscrutable and his strange, mismatched eyes—one blue and the other green—remained cool and distant. But that was how his friend had always been. He never showed any of his cards.

"Yes, your dad mentioned it, but everyone knows it was inevitable."

Lucas took a sip of the amber liquid from the glass in his hand. "Speaking of which ..." He motioned to the older man and woman standing in the middle of the room. "I think they're ready to make the announcement."

Zac followed Lucas' lead and moved closer to the vast penthouse's living room. As Alpha of New York and CEO of a multinational corporation, Grant Anderson could certainly afford to live in such a lush place. Not that he didn't know such luxuries himself; he grew up in the next building over in a similar apartment. Zac's father, after all, was the New York clan's Beta or second-in-command.

"Thank you everyone for coming here." Grant gazed down at his wife and Lupa, Frankie, beside him. "I know you all probably still have a hangover from the holiday parties and gatherings, so I appreciate you making the time."

This was an informal gathering for close friends and family, but still, there were over twenty people gathered tonight, including Zac's parents, and Grant's sister and brother-in-law, and of course, the various children who were still in town after the holidays or could make it, including two of Zac's own siblings.

Grant continued. "As you all know, I've been serving as Alpha of New York and CEO of Fenrir Corp. for over three decades now. Despite all the ups and downs, I wouldn't have had it any other way." He smiled down at his wife and then pulled her to his side. "But, as with many things, it must come to an end. I'll be making the formal announcement in a few days, but I wanted you all to be the first to know. I'll be stepping down as CEO of Fenrir Corp. as well as Alpha. And I'm naming Lucas as my successor."

Zac looked at his friend in disbelief. Grant had told him that he was stepping down as CEO, but not as Alpha. While it wasn't impossible, it was rare for an Alpha to abdicate, as the position was for life. Lucas' face remained impassive, though he took everyone's cheers and congratulations in stride.

"And to add to our big news for tonight, I'll be stepping down as Alpha of New Jersey as well," Frankie announced. "Adrianna will be taking my place."

Lucas' twin sister, Adrianna's mouth tightened into a line, though she answered the congratulations given to her graciously. When their eyes met, Adrianna sighed and shrugged her shoulders.

Zac raised his glass to her, and she rolled her eyes. *Interesting.* The New Jersey clan was matriarchal, and thus the title of Lupa was passed to the eldest daughter. However, since Frankie had married Grant, Adrianna and all her siblings grew up in New York.

With the Jersey clan growing, however, Frankie had to spend more time in her territory, which meant that Adrianna would most likely have to do the same, or even move there. For someone who grew up in Manhattan, moving to the burbs of Jersey was akin to a death sentence, which is probably why Adrianna didn't look ecstatic at the thought of becoming Jersey's Alpha.

"You look so serious, Zac. Penny for your thoughts?"

"For you, they cost nothing." Zac smiled at the petite redhead approaching him. "Enjoying the party, Mom?"

Cady Vrost smiled at her son. Even after all these years, she still looked young for her age—her hair remained a vibrant copper red and her green eyes sparkled with vitality. "I am."

A tall, blond man came up behind her and slipped an arm around her waist. "Well, if it isn't the most beautiful woman in the room." Cady laughed when he kissed her temple. "Son," Nick Vrost said. "I'm glad to see you here. You know you can stay with us whenever you're in town, right?"

"The hotel Fenrir puts me up in is fine," Zac said.

"Besides, it's not like I don't ever see you when I'm in town. We have dinner almost every other day."

"And all the other days?" Cady inquired. "Going on dates?"

"Sowing wild oats?" Nick added.

"If I'm sowing any oats, you won't be hearing about it," he answered. In truth, it had been a long time since he'd dated anyone. It's not that he didn't like women; he'd had plenty of experience when he was younger. But now, at the grand old age of thirty-one, sleeping around felt ... empty. Looking at his parents, the way they acted around each other, he couldn't help but feel envy for what they had.

Ridiculous, of course. Nick and Cady had something few had. For one thing, they were True Mates, a rare type of relationship with their kind. They were fated to be together, and although only two Lycans could produce another Lycan child, if at all, True Mates were different. Because they were destined to be together, such a pairing produced a pure Lycan child. He and his siblings were all pure Lycan, even though Cady was human. There were other things about True Mate pairings he had learned, but since it wasn't something on his radar, that particular lesson didn't really stick much in his mind.

"So," Nick said. "What do you think, son? Of Grant's announcement?"

"All this excitement," Cady added. "Change is coming, but I think it'll be good."

"So, what brought this about?" Zac asked. "Grant's not having some kind of late life crisis, is he?" As the New York

clan's Human Relations liaison and Grant's right-hand
woman, Cady Vrost knew anything and everything that
went when it came to both clan and Fenrir business.

She chuckled. "Nothing like that at all. But times have
changed, you know? Sure, the existence of Lycans is still a
secret from the human world, but it's not like the Middle
Ages when Lycans feared for their lives or had clan wars.
We're not even at war with the witches and warlocks.
We've had peace for the last few decades. Grant thought it
was time for new blood and to finally retire to that Italian
villa he and Frankie have been dreaming about for
so long."

"I suppose if anyone deserves some rest, it's them."
Still, this was an unprecedented move. The most powerful
Alpha and Lupa in the world retiring their positions. He
wondered how this would ripple through the rest of the
Lycan world.

Nick looked his son straight in the eyes. "They're not
the only ones."

His father was never one to waste words, so it was
pretty clear to Zac what he was implying. "You've never
mentioned anything about retiring." His father loved being
Beta and head of Fenrir Corp.'s security department, as
well as being in charge of the elite Lycan Guard who
protected the Alpha.

"Well, Grant and Frankie's decision got us thinking,"
Cady said. "It's all in the early stages, I assure you."

Nick gave him a meaningful look. "But since Lucas is

moving up to CEO, he's going to need someone to fill in his position as COO. Here in New York."

Ah, there it was. He and his father rarely butted heads; that was more his youngest brother Xavier's style. However, his decision to stay in London and become the head of the office there had rankled Nick Vrost. And he made no secret about wanting his eldest son to come home.

"This is all news to me," Zac said. "I haven't heard any offers."

"Well—"

"Nick," Grant called, waving his hand. "A moment, please."

"I'll be right back." He flashed Zac a look that said, *we're not done talking about this*, before walking toward the Alpha's direction.

"You know he wants the best for you." Cady placed a hand on his arm.

"I know." He covered her hand with his.

"We miss you a lot."

"I miss you too, Mom."

"And I know you miss *him*." Cady paused.

Zac squeezed his mother's hand, as if doing so would stop the way his chest tightened. "It's been five years."

"Vasili was special to all of us."

His father's grandfather, Vasili Vrost, had raised Nick when his parents died. The old man had been a big part of their lives, and he and Zac had been particularly close. When he passed away, it felt like a part of him died as well.

"Before I married your father, I lost someone too. My father. He was the only family I had at that point."

He had heard about his mother's father, Luther Gray, but Cady didn't talk much about his death. "Does it go away? The missing?"

"I'm still not sure." She gave him a sad smile. "But you know Vasili wouldn't have wanted you to leave because of him."

"I didn't," Zac said. Well, partly, but there were other reasons too. Speaking of which ...

"Zac," Nick was dragging Lucas along. "I was just telling Lucas our good news."

"You've served the New York clan as long as my dad has. Both of you." He pulled Cady in for a hug. "I was hoping you would both be here to guide me, but I understand your reasons, and you deserve to enjoy your lives too."

"We're not going away right away," Cady said. "We'll be here for your transition."

"But eventually you'll need to find someone to help you. A good Beta will ensure you can focus on more important things."

And there it was again. It was no secret that Nick had always hoped Lucas would pick Zac to be his Beta someday. It was a great honor of course, and Nick was the first of his family to be Beta. Unlike Alpha, which was a title passed from father to son, a clan's Beta was chosen. In the olden times, it was the strongest warrior, though these days the Alpha picked the best candidate based on his or her needs.

Lucas flashed Zac a meaningful look before clearing his throat. "No one knows that better than you, Nick. I look forward to receiving advice from both you and Cady when the time comes for me to choose."

"We'll be here." Nick took his wife's arm. "Cady, love, I think Alynna and Alex wanted to discuss something about dinner plans next week. Let's go and have a chat."

"Of course." Cady squeezed her son's arm. "I'll see you before you leave on Sunday?"

"We'll have dinner," Zac assured his mom. With that, Nick and Cady excused themselves and walked toward Alynna and Alex Westbrooke, who were chatting with Frankie and Adrianna by the fireplace.

"Why does this feel like a bad blind date?" Lucas asked with a raised brow.

Lucas never made jokes, so Zac was surprised to see the barely contained mirth in his friend's eyes. "Because it kind of is. Sorry, I hope I didn't put you on the spot."

"Not at all," Lucas said. "You know, if you don't want to be Beta, I could choose someone else. You don't even have to put your name in the hat."

"It's not that I don't want to be Beta," Zac began. "It's just ..."

"Feels like you don't have a choice in the matter?"

Despite being one of his oldest friends, Zac had never told Lucas his reservations about the position. But perhaps that's what made Lucas a natural leader—his ability to read those around him. "Being Beta was my father's life. He loved it. It was the one thing he had to earn, not one given to him because of his background or money."

"And you? You don't think you have to earn it?"

He laughed. "I know I have to earn it. And work at it. I'm just ..." What could he say? He had his reasons, but he wasn't quite ready to voice them out yet.

"Look, I won't choose you if you don't want it, Zac." Lucas' gaze bore into him. "But I would like you to consider taking over for me as Chief Operating Officer of Fenrir Corp., here in New York."

That was the next step in the career ladder for him, of course. "Let's talk about it another time. For now, go and have your moment in the limelight. Enjoy it."

Lucas frowned. "You know me better than that."

Zac smirked. Lucas hated the limelight even more than his father. "Right. Well I—" He stopped short when he saw one of the Lycan security guys briskly walk toward his father. The burly man leaned down and whispered in Nick's ear. His father frowned and said a few words back.

"Hold on," he said to Lucas, then made his way across the room. He wasn't sure why, exactly, but he felt a strange urge to find out what was wrong.

"Dad?"

Nick and Cady were speaking in hushed tones. "Yes, son?"

"Everything okay?"

His parents looked at each other. "It's fine, Zac," Cady said. "Clan business."

"Someone causing trouble." Nick's face was drawn into a scowl.

"Someone we know?" Zac asked.

"Oh yeah, we know her."

Cady shot her husband a warning look. "Nick. It's not like this is a regular occurrence." She turned to Zac. "Actually, maybe Zac would like to join us? See what it is we do?"

"Join you?" Zac asked. He knew what his mother and father did for the clan, of course, but he'd never actually been in the thick of the action.

"That's not a bad idea. What do you say, son?"

Zac supposed there was nothing to lose. "All right."

"Great." Nick took the phone out of his pocket. "I'll call Meredith. You guys tell Grant and Frankie that we're leaving a little earlier than expected."

"Meredith?" Zac asked. "Why does he need to call in his second-in-command? If this is dangerous—"

"Not at all," Cady assured him. "We need her for other reasons. C'mon, Zac. We should go as soon as possible."

CHAPTER THREE

M r. G told the girls to go back inside and get Petal cleaned up but act like nothing had happened. The one bouncer stayed behind and Mr. G handed him the gun and instructed him to keep an eye on Leon.

"Are your people coming?" he asked Astrid when she put the phone down.

"They'll be here in fifteen minutes."

His eyes narrowed at her. "Are you going to tell me what happened? And what you are exactly?"

"Uh, I'll wait until they're here," she said. "Please, Mr. G, will you trust me? Everything will be explained, I promise."

"Girly, I'm not even sure what I saw." He scratched at his balding head. "But we'll wait for your guys. You ain't mob, are you? Cuz I ain't getting mixed up in that crap."

I wish. "No, I swear I'm not."

As they waited in the alley together, Astrid prayed to any and every god and deity she could think of. *Please, please. Don't send* her. *Anyone but* her.

The minutes ticked by, and that dread in her stomach wouldn't go away. Finally, one of the bouncers walked out into the alley, followed by a familiar figure.

And maybe the gods were watching out for her that night, because when she saw the woman who walked into the alley, she sighed in relief.

"Astrid?" Cady Vrost said in a tentative voice. In the dingy alley, the cool, elegant redhead looked out of place in her Armani wool coat and Louboutin boots. "Are you all right?"

"I'm fine, Cady," she said. "Uh, long time no see?" Of course they would call Cady. As Human Liaison, it was her job to smooth things over if they ever got into trouble with humans.

"Yes, long time indeed." Her green eyes shifted over to Mr. G. "You must be Mr. Garavaggio. The owner of this, uh, establishment."

"Yeah, that's me." His brows drew together. "How did you know?"

"It's my business to know, I'm afraid," she said. "Now, tell me what—Astrid!"

She barely had time to react. A pair of meaty hands wrapped around her neck and pulled her back. She let out a strangled scream, then the wind knocked right out of her lungs when her back hit the wall.

Shit! Her vision began to turn white at the edges but

she could see who it was. Monroe. *Damn confounding potion!* Magic potions had to be brewed with a specific person in mind, to ensure it works for the right amount of time. The bottle she'd *liberated* from her father's cabinet must have been formulated for someone smaller than that hulking giant. She struggled against him, but her arms were feeling limp from the lack of oxygen.

Her vision was fading when she heard a low, animalistic growl. She thought she heard someone say, "get away from her" followed by a loud crash, but she wasn't sure. She slumped against the wall and slid down, gasping for breath and clawing at her neck.

When she could finally breathe, the scent hit her like a wallop to the nose. It was one of the most delicious things she'd ever smelled. Pine trees and something sweet; like walking in the woods and then being welcomed home with freshly-baked goods. Her she-wolf sniffed the air, breathing in the Christmassy scent, then let out a yowl. It whined with need, practically rolling on the ground from the amazing smell.

She blinked then looked up. Glowing eyes stared right back at her. It took her a few moments for her brain to unscramble but then she realized who it was.

Oh motherfreakin' fucknuts.

Zachary Vrost was the son of the New York clan's Beta and their human liaison. She and Zac were both born to the clan and attend many of the same functions, but it wasn't like they were childhood buddies or anything. Zac was not only older by a few years, but he was practically clan royalty. He came from one of the higher-ranking families, and thus he didn't exactly mingle with the common folk like her, despite their connection.

And, when she was younger—much younger—she *might* have thought she had a crush on him, but had always admired him from a distance. After all, their orbits were so far away, they might as well have lived on different planets. There was that one time she was foolish enough to think otherwise ... well, that was a whole other story. Besides, he was supposed to be living in London, as Fenrir's COO over there.

Which now begs the question, *what the hell was he doing here?*

The glow in his eyes began to dissipate, leaving behind a cool pair of ice blue eyes. He blinked and he looked just as surprised as she was. "Uh, Astrid, right?"

His voice was like soft velvet and she found herself unable to speak, so she just nodded. The years had been kind to Zac. No, they had been amazing—he looked like someone beat him up with a freaking handsome-as-sin-and-hot-as-hell stick. Several times. He'd always been tall, like his dad, but his shoulders were much broader, which strained against the suit he wore. He also sported just the right amount of designer scruff on his strong jaw, which added a hint of danger to his already handsome features.

"Are you okay?" He held out his hand. She stared at it for a moment, then took it. A soft gasp escaped her mouth when she felt the electricity zing across her skin when they touched. Did he feel that too? She didn't have time to check his reaction because he suddenly pulled her up. She was unprepared, so she stumbled forward. Strong arms wound around her to steady her, and she braced her hands on his chest.

Oh, God, were his muscles really that rock hard? *Better check again.*

"Uh, Astrid?" Zac's tone was bemused and she quickly stepped away from him when she realized she was caught squeezing his pecs through his shirt.

"Ahem."

She looked behind Zac. Oh fuck, her night couldn't possibly get any worse. "*Al Doilea.*" She bowed her head in respect as she called Nick Vrost by his formal title. "Er, so, how's it going?"

"How's it going?" The cutting tone in the Beta's voice was unmistakable. "Young lady, do you have any idea how much trouble you're in?"

"Dad." Much to her surprise, Zac put himself between her and his father. "She's hurt. That man attacked her."

"That man you sent crashing to the wall?" Nick said.

"He had his hands on her," Zac replied, his voice tight.

"It was my fault," Astrid said. "That confounding potion I used wasn't enough to keep him down."

Nick ran a hand through his hair. "Confounding potion? So, you not only shifted in front of humans, but you also used a magic potion?" The vein on his neck looked like it was going to pop any second. "Anything else I should know?"

"Well—"

"*Astrid!*"

She groaned and slapped a hand on her forehead. She was wrong; her night was going to get worse.

"*Astrid Ariel Jonasson!*" Meredith stopped right in front of her, so they stood toe to toe. With their similar height and features, many people often mistook them for sisters. "What is the meaning of this, young lady?"

Astrid rolled her eyes, a move Meredith hated. "It's nothing, Mom," she said.

"Nothing? *Nothing?*" She waved her hands in the air. "I get a phone call from Nick saying that you had called the Lycan security office for help and that I should rush home. What the hell are you doing here, and why are you dressed like that?"

"I work here." Oops. She realized she hadn't changed out of the peignoir, which was now partially open and showing a generous amount of cleavage.

"At a strip club?"

"It's a gentleman's club, Mom," she corrected.

Meredith's face fell and she looked like she wanted to cry. "Oh. My. God. You know those jokes comedians tell about how when they see a girl dancing on a pole and they think somebody's daddy fucked up with raising their child? Well, *I'm* that daddy!"

"Stop being so dramatic, Mom! I'm not a stripper! And they preferred to be called exotic dancers."

"What will your father say?" Meredith ranted. "And what do you mean you're not a stripper? Do they not think you're good enough? You're a hundred times more beautiful than any of the girls I saw in there."

"*Mom.*" Astrid wanted the ground to swallow her up. She was not doing this. Especially not in front of Zac Vrost and his father. "Look, it's a long story, okay? Are you done with the cleanup?"

"We're working on it," Nick said. "Cady's smoothing things over with the owner, and Daric's administering the forgetting potion to those who saw you shift."

"Dad's here too?"

"We were in Madrid, having these amazing tapas when Nick called us," Meredith said. "He transported us back right away."

Nick massaged his temple. "This is one big mess you left us, young lady," he said. "This is going to require an audience with the Alpha. Get your things and be ready to leave in five minutes." He turned to leave but stopped. "Zac?"

"Yes, Dad?"

"Are you coming?"

Zac shook his head. "Right. I'll uh, see you around, Astrid."

She stared after him as he followed Nick back inside the club. What the hell was Zac Vrost doing here anyway? Last she heard, he'd been living overseas in London. Did he move back to New York?

"Astrid. Astrid, are you listening to me?"

"What?" She whipped around to face her mother.

Meredith's expression softened. "Astrid, will you tell

me what's going on, please? What happened?"

"I was working—" She suddenly remembered Petal. "Mom! There's this girl. She was hurt pretty badly." Panic gripped her. She'd been so preoccupied that she didn't think about what happened to her friend. "Did they get her help? I told them to bring a doctor because I couldn't let them call 911 and—"

"That girl?" Meredith said, her expression going dark. "Yeah, I saw her. Don't worry, Dr. Blake is with her. He's treating her wounds now."

She breathed a sigh of relief. "Thank God."

Meredith looked over Monroe and Jamal, who had both been secured by members of the Lycan security team. One of the bouncers was leading Leon back into the club. "Did they have something to do with that girl getting beat up?"

Astrid nodded and gave her mother the short version of what happened. Meredith listened intently letting her talk.

When she was done, Meredith wrapped an arm around her shoulders. "You did the right thing, sweetie. It was stupid to shift and use your powers, but you were trying to help your friend and protect yourself."

"I know. But I had no choice." She bit her lip. "What's going to happen now?"

"You'll have to explain your side of the story to the Alpha," Meredith said. "But I'll be there to support you. And so will your father."

Astrid sighed. She was not looking forward to her audience with Grant Anderson.

CHAPTER FOUR

"Zac, did you hear what I said?"

His father's voice jolted him out of his daze. "Huh? I mean, what were you saying?"

Cady sent her son an amused smile as she turned her head back to him where he sat in the back seat of his father's Mercedes. After the excitement at the club, they had to come back to The Enclave to meet with the Alpha. "I hope you don't think this is something we have to do on a regular basis," she said. "I assure you, these days it's rare we even have to call the police chief when an incident like this occurs."

"Oh, so she doesn't cause trouble like this all the time?" he asked.

"Her?" Nick's brows furrowed. "Oh, you mean Astrid. No, she's not a troublemaker or anything. But I've heard stories."

"You know Meredith works closely with your father," Cady said. "And she's always talking about Astrid."

"More like complaining," Nick said. "She's not a bad kid, but she's obviously not focused or talented like her brothers."

"Nick," Cady admonished. "I'm sure Astrid has her other strengths. Not everyone can be like Cross Jonasson."

Ah, yes. Cross Jonasson. Zac knew all about the powerful hybrid—that is, half warlock, half wolf shifter— from Lycan and magical gossip. His own cousins from San Francisco were hybrids as well, and Cady was descended from a powerful line of female witches though she was fully human. But apparently, Cross was especially gifted, though he preferred to keep his talents a mystery.

They'd met several times over the years of course, but they didn't run in the same circles. Most Lycans lived in The Enclave, the clan's compound on the Upper West Side of Manhattan, but the Jonassons, along with the rest of their family, lived downtown. With his father, Daric, being a powerful warlock himself, they didn't need The Enclave's magical protection.

Zac wondered, however, if there were other reasons why his parents and the Jonassons never hung out socially nor did their children. Because if they did, he was pretty sure he would have noticed how beautiful Astrid Jonasson had grown up to be.

He had been initially perturbed that his father and mother's work brought them to a strip club downtown. It wasn't a seedy place, but it was obvious what was going on in there. And when they got to the scene, he saw that man approaching his mother and his instincts went into over-drive. The man didn't get to Cady, but instead went after the woman she was talking to.

Save her, something urged him. And so he grabbed the man and tossed him to the wall, barely containing his Lycan strength. His wolf gave a primal howl inside him, something he had never experienced before.

Then he looked into the depths of those whiskey-colored eyes and got lost. Who was this woman? The face was familiar and it all clicked into place. His mother and father were talking about her on the way here, after all.

His reaction to first seeing her still shook him to his very core. He racked his brain, trying to remember the child she had been. He recalled seeing her running around as a toddler at someone's—maybe his cousin's—birthday. As an awkward teen at Adrianna and Lucas' graduation. And maybe some Fenrir company picnics. But for the life of him, he didn't know why he hadn't seen her lately.

And here she was, dressed in that ridiculous red robe. The silk material clung to every luscious curve and the front gaped open to show him a generous hint of her breasts. With her golden hair tumbling down her shoulders she looked like some kind of siren, tempting him to come closer and ...

He shook his head. He wasn't a stranger to beautiful women, but Astrid seemed to have stunned him. Dumb-founded, he offered her his hand and the moment they touched, his skin lit up with electricity. As if it wasn't bad enough, when she stumbled against him, he felt her body press against his and he went instantly hard.

But it was her scent that drove him wild. Sweet, like the summer flowers that grew in his great-grandfather's Hudson Valley mansion. It sent his wolf on a frenzy, reveling in that scrumptious scent.

What was she doing here? Dressed like that, a dreaded feeling came over him. He wanted to tear something apart, knowing that other men had looked at her, probably wearing much less than she did at the moment. He felt this strange urge of possessiveness over a girl he hardly knew and could barely remember. It was a good thing Meredith arrived and his father had called him away, because God knows what he could have done.

"Zac?" Cady's voice shook him out of his reverie. "Are you all right, son?"

"Yeah."

"Then kindly stop destroying the upholstery? Your father just had them redone last week."

Zac looked down at his fingers, which had dug holes into the plush leather seat of the Mercedes. "Sorry, Dad." He gave his father a sheepish look through the rearview mirror. "Have them fix it, I'll pay you."

Nick harrumphed. "It's fine. We're here."

Zac looked around and realized they had arrived in one of The Enclave's private garages. He got out of the car and opened the door for his mother, and soon they were in the elevator and headed back into the Anderson's apartment.

Unlike when they had left, the Alpha's apartment

wasn't filled with people, and only the half-empty glasses and hors d'oeuvres platters scattered about were evidence that there had been a party at all. Most people were gone, except for the hosts, plus Adrianna and Lucas, who were seated on the couch with their mother. Grant Anderson stood in the middle of the room, a stern look on his face.

It seemed that the Jonassons had beaten them to the apartment, as Astrid was seated in front of the Alpha, Meredith behind her, an equally severe look on her face. Off to the side, silent as a stone, was Astrid's father—the powerful warlock, Daric. He leaned casually against the fireplace, his hands folded over his chest. When he turned to look at Zac and those eerie blue-green eyes landed on him, a strange sensation washed over him. He shook it off and followed his father and mother into the room.

"Now that we're all here," Grant began. "Anyone care to tell me what happened?"

"I received a call from the Lycan Security Officer in charge," Nick said. "Miss Jonasson called our hotline and explained that there had been an incident where she had accidentally exposed herself in wolf form to humans."

"And why would you do that, Miss Jonasson?" Grant said. "You know our laws."

"Of course I do," she said impatiently. "But it wasn't my fault."

"And whose fault was it?" Nick asked. "Why would you need to shift in such a place?"

"What place?"

"A strip club," Nick added.

"*Gentleman's club,*" Astrid corrected. "And if you just let me talk, I'll clear everything up."

"All right, then," Grant leaned down to look her in the eyes. "Talk."

"Well, you see, I was working—"

"Oh my God, do we have to talk about how my daughter works as a stripper—"

"Exotic dancer, Mom," Astrid interjected. "And for the last time. I. Am. Not. A. Dancer."

"Then what are you?" Zac suddenly said. All eyes turned to him, and he suddenly felt exposed for some reason.

"If you must know," she began. "I'm a bodyguard."

"Bodyguard?" Frankie asked. "Bodyguard for whom?"

"The dancers, of course." She took a deep breath. "Look, I got my part-time job at the library, but that's not exactly enough to pay my bills. So, I took on this extra job on weekend nights. Mr G.—that's the owner of The Vixen Den—hired me to look out for the girls. Not on the floor or anything, that's where he's got the bouncers, but some-times some of these slimeballs try to sneak into the dressing room and cause trouble for the girls. And at the end of the night, I walk the girls to their cars, Ubers, or the subway. I just put on my hoodie, and since I'm taller than most of them, I look like a guy."

"Okay, so we've established your employment," Grant said. "Tell us what happened tonight."

Astrid's demeanor changed. Zac could see how her body tensed and lips tightened into a thin line. "One of the girls, Petal, she had an old boyfriend sniffing around. She's been extra worried about him showing up at home or at work. She came in for her shift tonight, but I was late and I didn't see her. Then ..." She swallowed and her voice shook as she continued her story. "I found her outside. Those three men beat her up good and ... they said they were going to do things to her." Meredith's hand clamped down on her daughter's shoulders. "They came at me, and I defended myself. I knocked out one guy, and then used a confusion potion on the other." She glanced at her father and gave him an apologetic grimace. "But Leon—that's Petal's boyfriend—he pulled a gun on me."

"A gun?" Grant asked. "What happened?"

"I *poofed* out." She made exploding motions with her hands. "And then I ended up behind him and—"

"Hold on." Grant scratched his temple. "What do you mean, *poofed* out?"

"You know ... I *poofed*." She repeated the motions, spreading her fingers wide.

"Explain?"

She let out an exasperated breath. "Like this."

A soft pop filled the air and much to Zac's surprise, the only real way to describe the sound was indeed, *poof*. A moment later, she reappeared behind Grant. "And this."

Grant let out a growl and quickly spun around. Nick moved toward the Alpha, and so did Lucas. Zac knew why; the Alpha's wolf was taken aback by Astrid's sudden appearance that it sprang close enough to the surface for all of them to feel it. The ripple of power in the air was apparent, and Zac realized he had just witnessed the Alpha's power.

"I'm fine," Grant said, waving his son and Beta away. His eyes returned to normal, losing that glow all Lycans got when their wolves were making their presence known. "But, Miss Jonasson, please don't do that again."

"What the hell was that?" Lucas exclaimed. "Are you like Daric? You can transport across spaces too?"

"Only short distances," Astrid said. "The most I could do is maybe, six feet away? Right, Dad?"

The warlock nodded. "We experimented and that is about her maximum for now."

"Maximum?" Grant echoed.

"When she was about five, she started *poofing* through doors," Meredith said. "Scared the shit out of me when I was leaving the house and she just appeared by my feet."

"We bound her powers after that," Daric continued. "As we did all the hybrids, until they were old enough to start learning how to use their abilities. You all remember the accident Cross caused when he was just an infant."

"When I was about twelve, just before my first shift, Dad removed the binding spell," Astrid said. "He taught me how to use my powers. It works a little differently than his. I don't have to learn about anatomy or biology unlike him; I just seem to know how to transport my body. But I can't transport anyone with me like he does or move other things from one place to another."

"And did you use your powers to fight those men?" Adrianna asked.

"Er, not quite." She chewed her lip. "Uncle Connor taught me how to fight. I mean, he did for us all. My cousins and his kids, I mean. He insisted, especially us girls."

Frankie let out a whistle. "Wow. So, you can fight and *poof* from one place to another."

"You almost sound like a superhero," Cady said.

She shrugged. "It's not that special. I'm not even that high on the magical scale like Dad, or Cross, or even Gunnar."

"But she can kick ass," Meredith said proudly.

"Hmmm." Grant thought for a moment. "Well, this still doesn't erase the fact that you've caused us a lot of trouble. Daric had to use the forgetting potion on everyone who worked in the club."

"I'm sorry." Astrid placed her hands on her hips. "But I would do it again to help my friend."

"You could have done so much with your abilities," Nick said. "And you waste it all on a strip club?"

Astrid's brows raised all the way to her hairline. "Excuse me? Just because they're strippers, doesn't mean they don't deserve protection and respect!"

"You mean, exotic dancers?" Nick shot back.

"Whatever!" She suddenly slapped a hand over her mouth. "I—I'm sorry. That was disrespectful, *Al Doilea*."

"All right, all right." Grant waved a hand. "Everyone, calm down." He turned to Astrid, who went back to her original seat. "This still doesn't change the fact that you exposed our secrets to humans. And that means I have to report it to The Lycan High Council. And you must be punished."

Astrid opened her mouth to protest, but shut it when Meredith gave her a warning look. "I understand," she said meekly. "Are you sending me to the Lycan Siberian prison?"

"No." Grant folded his hands together. "Astrid Jonasson, I sentence you to a year in servitude to the Lycan clan."

"What?" Meredith and Astrid said at the same time.

"Oh, stop, Meredith," Grant said with a roll of his eyes. "This isn't like when you were sentenced to ten years for attempting to steal from us. No, Astrid will not be a prisoner or anything. But, she will train with the security team for a year. She will receive the same benefits and salary as any other trainee and work the same hours. You're still free to keep your other job or take any other job if you wish, as long as you don't expose us again."

"Wait, so you're giving me a job as punishment?" Astrid asked, astounded.

"Yes. You'll be working with Nick and your mother."

She slumped back in her chair. "I think I'll take my chances in Siberia."

"Oh, so working with me is a punishment?" Meredith murmured.

"You can't be serious, Grant," Nick said. "I don't have space for her in the team."

"Then make space," Grant ordered. "She'll only be a trainee. And if she chooses to stay, she has that option."

"Ha!" Astrid exclaimed. "Fat chance."

"I think it is an excellent idea." All eyes turned to Daric. "It will give my daughter a chance to learn discipline and maybe give her some direction."

"My team is not a boarding school, warlock," Nick bit out. Cady sent him a withering glare.

Daric remained cool and impassive. "I pledged to you, Grant, as did my mate, and my children were born of this clan." He bowed his head to Grant. "We have enjoyed the protection and privilege of the New York clan and live by Lycan law."

Astrid looked helplessly at her father, but then her shoulders dropped in defeat when he didn't say anything. She took a deep breath. "Alpha, I know Lycan law is final, and I accept the punishment."

"Excellent. Now, Nick will work out the details and I guess, I'll see you all Monday morning."

And that was their cue to leave. Everyone stood up and began filing out of the living room.

Even as Zac watched all of this unfold, he was still having a hard time digesting it. Astrid and her powers. And just in general, Astrid herself. She was a puzzle, a conundrum that his analytical mind wanted to solve. "Lucas," he called as he chased after his friend.

"Some night, huh?" Lucas said. "Are you leaving on Sunday? What time is the jet bringing you back to London?"

"Yeah, about that," Zac said. "I was thinking about what you said earlier in the evening ..."

Lucas's demeanor changed. "Wait. You mean about taking over as COO for Fenrir Corp.?"

He took a deep breath. "Yeah. I'd like to talk about it more. And the London office runs like clockwork, you know. I can be here and do my job, I'll just adjust my hours."

"Really?" Lucas gave him a suspicious look. "And about the other position? For my Beta?"

Zac paused. "I'd like to consider that too. Which is why I want to stay and ... learn the ropes, as they say."

"So, you're going to work alongside Nick, too?"

"It's the best way to learn."

Lucas patted him on the back. "Whatever you want. I know your parents would be thrilled that you're even thinking about it."

"I know." He glanced over at Nick and Cady, who were standing by the elevators. "I guess I'll tell them the good news."

As he walked over to his parents, he told himself he knew what he was doing. That staying in New York and possibly taking over for his father as Beta of the New York clan was the only reason he wanted to stay. As whiskey-colored eyes flashed in his mind, he brushed aside other thoughts that were creeping into his mind.

"Mom, Dad," he began. "I wanted to speak with you about something."

CHAPTER FIVE

The insistent sound of the alarm made Astrid groan. Her hand flew out from under the covers to knock the stupid clock off the bedside table.

"Serves you right," she grumbled. She threw the covers off her and then swung her legs over the side of the bed. What she really wanted to do was crawl back under the duvet, but she knew if she was even a minute late, her mother would chew out her ass. "God, I hate my life."

She got up from bed and trudged into the bathroom of her new home. Well, it was more like a dorm room, really; as part of her "punishment", she also had to live in the dorms with the other Lycan Security team trainees. Last night, her parents helped her move into the sixteenth floor of the Fenrir Corporation building, which served not only as the headquarters of the conglomerate, but also of most Lycan-related business in New York. "Oh God, I'm having flashbacks to when you guys brought me to my college dorm room," she had said.

"Maybe you'll actually last the entire year this time," Meredith shot back.

"*Skatten min*," Daric said, using the Norwegian term of endearment he had always used for his daughter. "It will be all right. Trust us on this one?"

"Besides, this place is way better than this rathole you shared with five people in Williamsburg," Meredith added.

"As least it was *my* rathole," Astrid grumbled.

"I used to live here, in the room down the hall. Right when I met your dad. Ooh, Daric!" Meredith sat on the bed and bounced up and down. "Doesn't this bring back memories?"

"Shoo!" she had shouted at her parents, pointing to the door. She did *not* want to hear about her parent's sex life, past or otherwise.

She got ready for her first day of training, putting on a pair of leggings, a sports bra, and a loose shirt. She slipped into a pair of sneakers before heading out to the common room where breakfast was being served. A few of the other trainees were lingering around, and she nodded at them in greeting before piling her plate high with food. As a Lycan, she had a healthy appetite, and since she was going to start physical training today, she knew she needed to keep her energy levels up. When she was done, she cleaned up her tray and headed down to the fifteenth floor where the gym and training rooms were. Upon arrival, she noted most of the trainees were there already, eighteen in total according to her count.

Being part of the Alpha's security team was a big honor. Lycan clans were dynastic and thus it was usually the ruling families who occupied higher positions in their society. Joining the Lycan Security Team was one way for anyone in the clan to move up, and with New York being one of the biggest and most prestigious clans, Lycans from all over the state and country were vying to be part of this particular team. There was a good number of transferees—Lycans from other clans—this time around, and much to Astrid's surprise, about half of the trainees were women. Of course, New York was one of the more liberal clans, and Astrid's own mother was second-in-command of the entire team.

Speaking of which, her mother was already waiting at the front of the room, where the other trainees were assembled in front of her.

"You're late," she said, a stern look on her face.

"I'm on time." She pointed to the clock on the wall. It was exactly eight o'clock.

"If you're on time, you're already five minutes late," Meredith retorted.

"Fine," she said. "Where do you want me."

"Just go to the end of the line and—oh." Meredith's back stiffened. "*Al Doilea.* I wasn't expecting you today."

Everyone in the room turned around. Nick Vrost walked into the training room, and much to Astrid's surprise, Zac was right behind him.

"Good morning," he said. "I thought I'd drop in today to check on the progress of the recruits. He gestured to his son. "You all know my son, Zachary. He'll be staying in New York for the next few weeks, and seeing as he may be considering a new position in the company, I thought it best to show him the ropes."

"Please, don't let me get in your way," Zac said. "Pretend I'm not here."

"Anyway," Nick continued. "We also have someone new on the team. Miss Jonasson will be joining you for the next twelve months."

"Miss Jonasson will have to catch up on the training, seeing as she's behind," Meredith said, her face remaining neutral. "But she will be expected to perform to the best of her abilities, just like everyone else."

It was clear what her mother was trying to say: Astrid was not getting any special treatment just because she was related to her. Not that she was expecting it.

"All right," Meredith said, taking out her clipboard. "Let's begin with drills, shall we?"

The first hour of drills was grueling, and by the time two hours had passed, rivulets of sweat poured down Astrid's forehead and neck, soaking her shirt. Just as her mother threatened, she was not given any special treatment; if anything, Meredith was harder on her than anyone else. Still, she gritted her teeth and took it, vowing to herself that no one was going to break her, especially not her mother and not under the gaze of Zac Vrost.

Even as she went through the various drills, she still

couldn't get Zac out of her mind. She could have sworn she felt him looking at her, but she wasn't sure as she couldn't just stop and check. God, she must look terrible too. She was sweating like a pig and her shirt was plastered to her back. Her ponytail had gone askew, but she didn't even have time to breathe, much less fix her hair.

Stop it, she berated herself. She'd never cared about her looks before, so why start now?

"All right," Meredith said after she blew the whistle hanging from her neck. "Ten-minute break."

Her legs felt like jelly as she practically crawled to the water fountain. Lycans were stronger and faster than humans, but they weren't invincible. They still got tired, and these exercises and drills were designed just for Lycans.

"Not bad, new girl." A petite but buff girl handed her a cup of water. "I'm Layla. Jones."

"Thanks." Astrid took the cup and downed it in seconds. "Astrid." She held out her hand and the other Lycan gripped it tight.

"I know who you are." Layla looked at her from head to toe. "And I know why they rest of us are here. But, are you a sadist or something? Got Mommy issues?" She snuck a peek over at Meredith, who was chatting with Nick.

Astrid laughed. "Something like that."

Layla straightened her shoulders. "Well, I'd understand if you dropped out." The other woman was about five inches shorter than her, but it was obvious what she was doing. Posturing and asserting her dominance. Miss Jones was obviously in it to win it.

I wish I could drop out. "Don't worry." Astrid grabbed a towel from the rack next to the fountain and wiped down her face. "I won't be taking anyone's spot on the team. I'm just here as punishment. Alpha's orders."

Layla visibly relaxed. "Ah, so you're here under duress."

"Yeah, no choice. Believe me, I'd leave if I could. And I will when my time here is done."

She chuckled. "Well then, I guess we can be friends."

"Break's over!" Meredith called. "Everyone, to the mats."

They hurried over to the sparring mats, where everyone stood to the side, leaving a large space in the middle.

"So, is that guy your boyfriend or something?" Layla asked.

"Who?"

"The Beta's kid." Layla gestured to Zac with a nod.

"What?" She felt heat creep up her neck. "Why do you say that?"

"Because he's looking at you like he wants to eat you." She wiggled her eyebrows at her. "And by eat you, I mean—"

"I think I know what you mean." Heat bloomed in her cheeks. Was Layla serious? "And no, I don't even know him ... that well."

"Well it looks like he wants to get to know you."

Before she could say anything, Meredith blew her whistle to get everyone's attention. However, it was Nick who spoke. "I've been speaking with Meredith and she told me that you've all been doing well on improving your fighting techniques," he began. "You're all here because you're the best and we need only the best on the security team. Protecting the Alpha, his family, and the clan is of utmost importance." He paused. "You've all studied Lycan history, as well as recent history. Maybe some of your parents or family members fought in the Battle of Norway." There was silence in the group. Beside her, Layla tensed and her lips pursed together tightly. Astrid knew all about the Battle of Norway. It was fought in her father's childhood home, after all.

"Anyway," Nick continued. "Just because we've vanquished our enemies, doesn't mean that we will never encounter them or any type of magic again. Later in the year, you'll be taught by some of our witch and warlock allies about types of magical potions and ailments, and how to combat them. However, I thought it might be interesting for you to get an early start on your magical training. Especially since we have someone on the team who can help us out."

Oh, no. Astrid wrung her hands together. She hoped he wasn't going to do what she thought he was going to do.

"Miss Jonasson," Nick said. "Come up, please."

Layla shot her a confused look. "What's going on?"

"Er, I'm not sure." She walked to the front. "*Al Doilea,*" she began before he said anything. "I respectfully decline. I've been taught that my talents are not tricks for anyone to exploit."

"She's right," Zac piped in. "Leave her alone."

Nick ignored his son. "Part of your punishment is to work like any member of this team. And so, you must obey."

"Mom?" Astrid turned to Meredith.

"It's all right." Meredith leaned over and gave her a squeeze on the shoulder, then leaned down to whisper in her ear. "Show them what you got."

Astrid saw something rare flash in her mother's eyes—pride. Growing up, Uncle Connor and her mother had taught her to fight, but said that it was always to defend herself. Daric was very protective of his children and their abilities, and thus he always taught them to keep it hidden as much as possible, for their own protection. To use both now seemed like she was doing something bad, but apparently, Meredith was all for it.

"All right then," she said, cracking her knuckles. "If you say so."

"Jones," Meredith called. "You're up first."

Layla stepped forward. "You want me to spar with this skinny white girl? Your kid?"

"Like you would anyone," Meredith said.

"Fine. Whatever."

She and Layla faced each other on the mat. Layla's body was stiff and her face was drawn into a dour expression. "Are you okay?" Astrid began.

"My mom died in Norway." Layla stretched to full height and shook out her arms.

"I'm sorry," she said. "Maybe we should—"

"Go!" Meredith said.

Astrid didn't anticipate the match starting so soon and in a split second, she found herself splayed out on the mat, staring at the ceiling, the air rushing from her lungs. "Oomph!"

"Better pay attention next time," Layla taunted. "Or else—hey!"

Astrid used a leg sweep to knock Layla off her feet. "Oh, I'm paying attention," she said, looking down at the other girl.

Layla kicked out her legs, quickly getting to her feet. "You're not going to get me off guard again."

She motioned for Layla to come at her. "Give me your best shot."

When Layla lunged at her, Astrid did what she knew Nick and Meredith wanted her to do. *Poof.* She reappeared six feet away, and Layla tumbled to the ground.

The trainees let out a collective gasp, followed by various reactions ranging from "Oh my God" to "What the fuck was that?"

"Holy shit!" Layla shot to her feet. "What in God's name just happened?"

Astrid's shoulders slumped. She thought of Petal, and her reaction to her powers. *So much for having friends.* This year was going to be very long.

Layla came over to her, and Astrid was ready for the

derision she would face. After all, if Layla's mother died in Norway, she probably hated what she was.

"That was awesome," Layla said, her mouth spreading into a smile.

"It was?"

"Yeah, girl! I've never seen anything like it."

Huh.

"Miss Jones, Miss Jonasson." Nick's brows drew together. "Can we continue?"

"Let's go," Layla said. "And don't you hold back on me."

———

Astrid didn't think she'd be having so much fun on the first day of her punishment, but she was. It was actually freeing, being able to use both her combat skills and her abilities. Uncle Connor had never asked her to use her teleporting abilities while they sparred, and perhaps this was something she could show him during their next session. She saw him at least once a month, training with her cousins to keep their skills fresh. He insisted on it, and he would hound her if she missed a session.

Most of the other trainees seemed to accept her and enjoyed sparring with her. Well, most of them anyway. There were definitely a few who were frustrated that they couldn't even grab her.

"This isn't fair," Frank, a mouthy Lycan from Long Island, growled when Astrid disappeared from his grasp.

"How are we supposed to fight something we can't even touch?"

"You'll have to figure it out," Meredith said. "That's part of your training. Not everyone is invincible. Every opponent has a weakness. You need to be smart enough to find it."

"She's a witch," another trainee said. "And a Lycan. I don't think she has a weakness."

"She does."

Everyone's head whipped around. Zac was leaning casually against one of the treadmills.

"What is it?" Layla asked.

"Yeah, do tell, Zac." Astrid planted her hands on her hips. Who the hell did he think he was? He wasn't even part of the team, just observing. She puffed out her chest. She was trained by the *motherfucking feral wolf* of New York. Her father was the most powerful warlock in the world.

"Maybe I can show you instead?" Zac loosened his tie, took it off, and then removed his jacket, draping both over the side of the treadmill.

Astrid looked to Meredith and Nick, waiting for them to say something. "I think it's a great idea," Meredith said.

Okay, that was not what she was expecting her mother to say. "Fine." She wiped the floor with every single one of these trainees. Surely, she could do the same with some Oxford-educated executive. "I'm not going to go easy on you," she warned him. *Even if you do look hot in just your white shirt.*

"I don't expect you to, Astrid." He walked toward where she stood in the middle of the mat. The muscles of his shoulders strained against the fabric. When he rolled up the sleeves to his elbows, Astrid had to stop herself from drooling when she saw the ink. *Jesus H. Christ on a bicycle*, tattoos were one of her number one weaknesses when it came to men. Standing this close, she could scent him, and she could barely contain her wolf.

"All right then." She pushed those feelings of desire away. This was Zac Vrost, for God's sake.

"Do your worst."

Astrid treated Zac the same way she did with the other recruits. She sparred with him hand-to-hand first. She had to admit, he was good. Of course, he was the son of the Beta, so he knew how to fight. Karate, most likely. Maybe some jiu-jitsu. She let him think he had the upper hand a few times—something she learned from Meredith. *Let their guard down, then strike*. When Zac made a grab for her, she knew it was time to shut this down. She *poofed* and relocated herself just behind him, to his left.

"I—hey!" For only the second time that day, Astrid found herself on her back. But this time, a very hard and very male body was on top of her. "What the—" A hand came over her eyes, and her vision went dark. *Motherfucker!*

In her blinded state, it was like the rest of her senses went into overdrive. This close, his scent was even stronger, permeating her very being. The hard planes of his body pressed down on her. She squirmed, trying to get him off her, but he only bore down, trapping her by locking her knees between his. She gasped when she felt something hard brush against her stomach and a flood of desire pooled between her legs. He let out a surprised gasp and rolled away from her.

She blinked. What the hell—

"Astrid?" Meredith stood over her, looking down at her. "Are you all right?"

There was nothing like seeing your mother to totally douse your on-fire libido. "Yeah, um." She took the hand Meredith offered and hopped to her feet.

Nick stood to the side, barely containing his smirk. "Care to tell us her weakness?"

Zac was running his fingers through his blond locks. "What?" He looked confused, his eyes glazed over.

"What did you observe, son?"

Zac cleared his throat, then addressed the rest of the trainees. "Astr—Miss Jonasson has a tell," he began. "Right before she uses her power, she looks toward the direction of where she wants to reappear. I suspected that she needs to calculate precisely where she wants to go and needs a clear line of sight."

Sonofabitch. How the hell could he have known? It was one of the limits of her power, as she and her father discovered. She had to see where she was going or at least have been in the space before.

"She looked over my left shoulder, and so I simply guessed that's where she would be."

"And you were right," Nick said, the pride in his voice unmistakable.

"I also covered her eyes so she wouldn't be able to disappear while I subdued her."

Astrid felt her face grow hot. "Lucky guess, then."

Zac didn't even look at her. "An educated guess, but my advantage was that I had to watch all of you fight her before I could put it to the test."

"So," Nick began. "As we've always told you, fighting is ..."

As Nick continued his lecture, Astrid continued to stew, her hands turning to fists at her side. *Stupid Zac Vrost.* "So, is this why I'm here? To be humiliated?" she asked Meredith.

"You shouldn't have been so cocky," she shot back. "Have you forgotten your training with us? You never get too confident and you never let your guard down."

Ouch. That certainly stung. But she had to admit her mother was right. She glanced over at Zac again, and this time, his blue eyes were trained right on her. She held his gaze, daring him to look away. That heat she felt when she was under him spread through her body again, and this time, she was the one who had to turn away. It was too intense, and he was making her feel things she shouldn't.

"C'mon," Meredith said. "Let's get back to work."

CHAPTER SIX

After Monday's exercise, Zac never showed up again during training. And, despite the fact that she told herself *"good riddance"*, Astrid still felt that disappointment in the pit of her stomach each day she showed up for training and he wasn't there.

Ugh. The things he made her feel was disturbing. At night, she'd lie awake thinking of him and how his body felt against hers. She was still wondering if she'd imagined it, or that last bit when she felt his surging erection against her. *He's a guy.* If Zac felt anything it was because it was a natural function of the male body.

Still, it wasn't good for her sleep or her sanity. She'd only had three hours of sleep that night, that's why she was grumpy when she answered the phone call that came in at about seven o'clock that morning.

"What do you want?" she groused.

"Why didn't you tell me you were living at Fenrir?" came the very annoyed voice of Deedee Creed.

"Hey, Deedee," she said casually.

"Don't 'Hey, Deedee' me." Her best friend really did sound genuinely mad. "I had to hear from my mother, who heard from your mother, that the Alpha is punishing you for a whole year. Why didn't you call me?"

Astrid rolled over and pulled the covers above her head. "I've been busy, okay? I'm sorry."

"Sorry isn't good enough," Deedee said with a sniff. "I want details."

"Fine."

"Over dinner."

And so that night, Astrid found herself walking into *Petite Louve*, a French restaurant in the trendy SoHo district in downtown Manhattan. Deedee was already sitting at the table when she arrived.

"Astrid!" she greeted as she stood up to hug her. Although Deedee was five years older than her, they had become best friends over the years. She was like the older sister she'd never had and probably one of the few people around her who knew the awkwardness of having a five-inch growth spurt at the age of fourteen.

"How's life, Distinguished Professor Creed?" she teased. After she finished her PhD in London three years ago, Deedee came home and became a professor of Archeology at New York University. Just last week, however, she had been named a Distinguished Professor at NYU to honor her achievements in the field. "So, does everyone have to bow down to you when they pass you in the hallways?"

"Ha, I wish. But it's nothing more than just a fancy title, plus a grant for me to pursue any type of research I want to do." They sat down at the cozy two-top in the corner of the restaurant. "And as much as I'm sure you're interested to hear about how I'm planning to study the migration patterns of the ancient people of Mesopotamia, we're here to talk about you." Deedee flashed her that *I'm-disappointed-in-you* big sister look she'd perfected over the years.

"Can we order first? I'm famished." She opened the menu, but the gesture was more to hide from her friend, as she already knew every single dish there.

"Finc," Dee said. "But once we're done, you're going to tell me why I, *your best friend*, was the last to know about this life changing news."

"Oh, stop being so dramatic, Dee. I'll tell you, okay?"

After they'd finished ordering and the waiter was barely two feet away, Deedee laid her hands on the table and said, "Talk."

Astrid let out a sigh and gave her the entire story from start to finish, leaving out *one tiny detail*. Deedee was actually the only person who knew about her working at The Vixen Den, and Astrid realized she had been remiss in her best friend duties for not telling her right away. Though they tried to talk every day and get together as often as possible, Deedee was always so busy with her job and tended to lose track of time, and sometimes even the days.

Plus, Astrid was always changing jobs, it wasn't even a topic of conversation for them anymore.

"But this isn't exactly a job," Deedee pointed out. "This is punishment. It's going on your record for the rest of your life."

"Oh, for God's sake, Dee, you've always been such a goody-goody." She grabbed a piece of bread and buttered it before popping it in her mouth. "Those records at the Lycan High Council are meaningless."

"So, what are you going to do now?" Deedee asked.

"Ride out the year," she said. "And then move on with my life."

"Hmm ..."

Astrid put her butter knife down. "And what exactly do you mean by *hmm,* Miz Desiree Desmond Creed?"

"Nothing." She took a sip of her sparkling water. "It's just ... maybe this could be a good thing for you."

"What? Being punished is a good thing?"

"No!" Deedee put her hands up. "Astrid, I love you. You're one of my bestest friends in the whole wide world. But do you know how many jobs you've had in the last four years?"

"I dunno. Five? Six?"

"Eighteen."

"I did not!"

"Yes, you did."

"That time I was a living statue in Times Square doesn't count."

Deedee sighed. "Anyway, my point is, maybe this is

good for you. A job that you can't really quit. It'll give you—"

"Direction?" Astrid finished. She sat back and crossed her arms over her chest. "Why don't you just join my mother's side then?"

"*Astrid.*" She reached over and placed a hand on her arm. "I'm on your side, okay? Whatever happens. I've upset you, I'm sorry. We can talk about something else."

"You know you can never upset me, Dee," she said. "I just ... this was just a couple days ago, okay? I'm still figuring things out."

"All right. We can talk about something else. But you're not trapped at Fenrir, are you? You'll still make it to my party tomorrow, right?"

"Oh shit, is that tomorrow?" This was the party to celebrate Deedee's promotion. She didn't want one, but it was actually Deedee's mother, Aunt Jade, who'd convinced her she should celebrate her accomplishments. "I still have to do a shift at The Vixen Den." She didn't want to give up her job as a bodyguard because the girls needed her. She was only able to convince Nick and her mother to let her keep it because A, it worked with her training schedule and B, she reasoned that although the forgetting potion worked on making everyone lose their memories of her using her powers and shifting, it might seem strange if she suddenly just disappeared.

"It's not till late," Deedee said. "It was kind of a last-minute thing, and not everyone can come for dinner. So, I'm having supper with my parents first and then inviting everyone to come to Blood Moon after. My mother had the VIP room reserved for me."

"Oh good, I'll be there for sure."

The waiter arrived with their appetizers, and the tension between them dissipated. However, as they enjoyed their escargot, Astrid couldn't help but notice her friend looking around her nervously. Dee's eyes darted around and she fiddled with her napkin a lot.

"All right, Dee. Your turn."

Deedee's light green eyes looked up at her. "Am I that transparent?"

"Yes."

"It's nothing, I mean ..." She wiped her mouth with her napkin. "I was wondering ... have you seen Cross lately?"

Ah yes. Her MIA oldest brother. Before Astrid had been born, it was Cross and Deedee who had been attached at the hip. But Astrid's arrival didn't cut in on their friendship; in fact, it had only strengthened it, and over the years, they had been an inseparable trio.

Eventually, all of them grew up and had their own lives. Deedee went off to London, Cross remained in New York, and Astrid was ... well, she was being herself. Still, they had always kept in touch and spent as much time together as they could, especially since Deedee returned to New York. Cross' withdrawal from his sister and best friend had been more of a recent phenomena.

"You know he's been kinda ... weird the past year," Astrid said.

"And he hasn't talked to you or anything?"

"Nothing of note." Come to think of it, it had been a while since she'd seen or anyone even mentioned Cross.

"Oh." Deedee looked down at her lap.

This time, it was Astrid who reached over to Deedee. "Are you going to tell him?"

"Tell him what?"

"That you've nursed this crush on him since you were sixteen?"

"What?" Her eyes widened and a blush spread over her cheek. "I have not."

"Please, Deedee, it was so obvious." Astrid said. "Our moms thought it was cute."

"Well, I can't believe you're only telling me now that everyone knew." Deedee pouted. "Anyway, that was more than ten years ago and I am *not* crushing on him anymore. I'm just concerned as I haven't heard from him for a while. You know he didn't even show up for our traditional Christmas dinner."

"I know," Astrid said. "I'm sure he had his reasons. But, well ... maybe you could tell him how you feel next time you do see him? You did invite him to your party, right?"

The blush deepened on her cheeks. "I did. He said he'd try. But I can't say anything. I mean, I don't feel that way anymore."

"Oh please, Deedee! What could it hurt? You know, our moms would be over the moon if you guys started dating and then got married and had babies—"

"No. It could never happen," she said firmly. "We're just friends. And maybe he won't even show up."

Astrid eyed her friend carefully. Did Deedee have deeper feelings for Cross than she made it sound like? "Dee, come on. I would be thrilled too—that means we'd really be sisters."

"Astrid you know—oh!" Dee pointed behind her. "Look who's here!" She waved her hand. "Zac! Zac, over here."

Oh, no. Astrid covered her face with her hands. *Maybe it was a different Zac?* She grabbed another piece of bread and stuffed it in her mouth. *Fat chance.* Her inner wolf was practically beaming as it scented Zac Vrost. *Oh, shut it, you stupid animal.*

"Deedee," Zac greeted as he came closer. When his eyes landed on Astrid, he seemed just as surprised as she was.

"Zac, you remember Astrid? Aunt Meredith's youngest kid?" Deedee said.

"I do," Zac said curtly. "Actually, we've been reacquainted this weekend."

Deedee's eyes narrowed at Astrid. "You have?"

"Yes, I saw her at her, uh, place of employment." Zac said in a bemused voice. "Old and new."

"She never mentioned about you being there." Deedee looked daggers at Astrid. "Did you, best friend of mine?"

Okay, so that was the *one tiny detail* she didn't tell Deedee. "Oh, did I forget to mention that Nick and Cady had brought Zac along? And that he was there for my first day of training?"

Deedee smirked. "Yes, you did forget to mention that fact."

"Well, he was," Astrid said nonchalantly. "End of story."

Zac looked at her strangely, then turned to Dee. "So, how have you been, Deedee? It's been a while since London."

"After graduation, I went to...."

As Deedee gave him a rundown, Astrid wanted to kick herself. She forgot that Deedee and Zac had studied in London at around the same time, so of course they were friends too.

"—and the job's been great," Deedee finished. "So, are you here alone? Want to join us for dinner?"

Astrid wanted to scream *no* at Deedee but kept a tight smile on her face.

"Actually, I'm just here to pick up an order before I go back to my hotel."

She breathed a sigh of relief.

"But I'm sure I could ask the waitstaff to plate my meal so I can sit down with you."

Oh crap.

"Sounds like a plan. We'll wait right here while you go talk to them," Dee said sweetly. As soon as Zac was out of earshot, her gaze narrowed at Astrid. "Speaking of childhood crushes ..."

"Oh, shut your dirty mouth." Astrid tossed a piece of bread at her. "That was years ago."

"Five years ago. Hannah's wedding."

Astrid cringed at the reminder. "Which only proved my point: he didn't even know I existed back then."

"Right." Dee brushed an imaginary piece of lint from her blouse. "So, tell me the entire story this time."

Astrid knew she didn't have a choice, so she filled in the details of how Zac fit into everything. She tried to pass it off as casually as she could without giving any hint of what had passed between them. Because, as far as she was concerned, there *was* nothing between them.

"Oh, my. Do you think Zac's going to be the next Beta?"

Hmm, she hadn't even considered that. "It seems logical, I guess. He is Nick's son."

"It's not that logical," Deedee said. "The position of Beta isn't passed on, like Alpha. Oh wait, shush, here he comes and—uh-oh."

"Uh-oh? What do you mean, *uh-oh*?"

"Zac's coming back, but he's not alone."

Astrid looked behind her and saw who else was headed their way. *Fucknuts.* "The twins."

Isabelle Anderson and Maxine Muccino weren't really twins; they were actually first cousins as Isabelle's mom, Frankie, and Maxine's dad, Dante, were siblings. But, the two of them might as well have been twins because they looked so similar—same height, same petite frame, and the same mismatched blue and green eyes that everyone descended from the New Jersey Alpha shared. Both were also vapid and vain, and at one point, made Astrid's life a living hell despite being younger than her.

"Hey, Dee!" Isabelle greeted. "Oh, and ... Astrid? Astrid Jonasson?" The tone of her voice sounded like she had smelled days-old fish.

"Hello, Maxine. Isabelle," Astrid said with a tight smile. Isabelle Anderson had been particularly mean to her, mocking in particular, her dismal fashion sense. As the daughter of a billionaire Alpha, Isabelle was always dressed from head to toe in the latest designer outfits. "Nice to see you here."

"Well, we wanted to see Mama and Dominic," Maxine said. Her mother, Holly Muccino, owned *Petite Louve,* and her oldest brother ran the kitchen on most days.

"But we ran into Zac, isn't that nice?" Isabelle placed a hand on his arm. "And we thought, we should sit down to dinner together."

Isabelle's fingers stroking Zac's arm really shouldn't have bothered Astrid, but it *did.* She had to rein in her she-wolf, who was now gnashing its teeth at her.

"All of us," Zac added.

"But this table is so tiny." Isabelle pointed to the two-top Deedee and Astrid were sitting at.

Zac looked around the half-empty dining room. "It's not too busy, I'm sure the waitstaff could put us at a larger table, right, Maxine?"

"Of course," the girl replied cheerfully, which earned her a pointed look from Isabelle. "Er, let me go talk to the maître d'."

After a bit of shuffling around, all five of them were

seated at a larger, circular table, and Astrid found herself seated to Zac's right with Isabelle on the other side.

"Nice shirt, Astrid," Isabelle looked her up and down. "Did you get it at a vintage store? They seem to be popping up everywhere these days."

She looked down at the pink T-shirt with the faded logo for an old bubblegum brand. "As a matter of fact, I did."

"You're so forward-thinking. You've always shopped at Goodwill, even when we were younger." She flipped her hair and laughed.

Astrid felt a firm grip on her right wrist. When she looked down, she saw Deedee's fingers around her hand which was already gripping a fork. When she dropped the fork and put her hand on her lap, Deedee released her.

"My mother was very practical," Astrid said.

"And it's not like you grew up without money," Zac added. "You had that awesome loft in Tribeca. It was a converted warehouse, right? Uncle Sebastian owned half, and Meredith and Daric bought the other half. I remember going there for someone's birthday, probably Deedee's."

"True," Astrid said. "But when I was younger, I asked my mom if we were rich. She replied, 'Well, *I'm* rich, *you're* poor. Everything you have was bought with *my* hard-earned money.'"

Zac threw his head back and laughed. "Isn't that the truth."

Isabelle squirmed in her seat which Astrid counted as a win, though for what, she didn't know. When she smirked at the younger woman, Isabelle's nostrils flared, but she pasted a smile on her face. "Zac, I forgot to tell you, do you remember that old man who lived in your building? Mr. Smith?"

"Yes, I remember."

"I have the most hilarious story to tell you," she tittered. "I was walking Fifi the other day and...."

As the meal progressed, Isabelle masterfully manipulated the conversation so only she, Maxine, and Zac could participate. Astrid told herself it was okay, and she didn't really want to chat with them anyway. Deedee glanced at her with a concerned look on her face, but Astrid shrugged and instead, dug into her delicious beef bourguignon, eating up every morsel. Stuffing herself with food felt like a good idea right now.

Finally, dessert was served, and when the check was paid, they all got ready to leave.

"Zac," Isabelle said in a low whisper. "Maxine and I were going to check out this awesome club in the Meatpacking district. You should totally come with us."

"And Astrid and Deedee too, right?" he said.

"Why not?" Deedee pulled at Astrid's arm. "Let's go."

"I didn't know you liked to go clubbing, Deedee," Maxine said.

Astrid looked at Deedee. "You hate clubs."

"What? I can't change my mind?" Her grip on Astrid's arm tightened. "C'mon."

She knew what Deedee was trying to do, but she wasn't having any of it. If Isabelle Anderson wanted Zac

Vrost, then she could have him. It was obvious anyway that the young woman had her sights set on him. And why not? She was young and the Alpha's daughter, and soon he would be Beta, and they'd be such a perfect Lycan power couple it made Astrid want to throw up.

She pulled her hand away from Deedee's grasp. "You guys have fun. I have early training tomorrow, and it's pretty grueling."

Zac began to protest. "Astrid—"

"It's fine." She waved her hand at them. "I'll see you all soon. Bye now." She didn't waste any time and grabbed her jacket from the back of her chair, then ran out the front door. She had barely put one arm inside her jacket when she heard the restaurant door open.

"Astrid. Astrid!"

"*Shit biscuits*," she muttered under her breath. She supposed she could keep going, but she couldn't exactly pretend she didn't hear him. "Yes?" She spun around.

"Hold on." Zac caught up to her. "Where are you going?"

"Back to Fenrir," she said. "Like I said, I have an early day."

"Let me take you there, then," he offered.

"What about Isabelle?"

He sent her a blank look. "What about her?"

"Aren't you going clubbing?"

He chuckled. "Me, clubbing? I'm not twenty-one anymore."

"But you were ... you said."

"Did I say 'yes, I'm going clubbing'?"

"Er ..." She bit her lip. "I guess you didn't."

"My car's this way." He took her hand, and when the electricity from his touch made her skin come alive, she jumped back.

"No!" she cried. "I mean ..."

"Astrid," he said in a low voice. The air around them became still and quiet. He took one step forward and she took one back. They repeated this until she found herself pressed up against the wall behind her.

"Zac?" she whispered, afraid to look up at him. He tipped her chin up, and she had no choice but to peer up at his ice blue eyes. They had grown dark now and he was leaning down and—

Poof.

When Astrid opened her eyes, she was back inside *Petite Louve* and had reappeared in front of a waiter carrying a tray laden with dishes. The woman shrieked as the plates of food crashed to the floor.

"S-s-sorry! I'm so sorry!"

Mortified, she turned tail and headed out the back door, her heart hammering in her chest. The cool air hit her face like a wallop when she burst through the rear door and ran into the alley that led to the dumpsters.

Oh God. She kept running, not really caring where she went, as long as it was far away from Zac Vrost.

ac knew all about the five stages of grief, but right now, he was wondering if there was such a thing as five stages of *what the fuck just happened?* Because in the span of about ten seconds, he went from surprise, to disbelief, to denial, to anger, until he finally accepted that she was gone.

He ran back into the restaurant, figuring that's where she'd be but didn't find her. As he carefully stepped over a pile of broken dishes and food some poor, clumsy waiter must have dropped, he stalked back to the table where the three remaining ladies were waiting.

"Where is she?" he asked Deedee.

"Who?"

"Astrid." He gritted his teeth.

"Um, I don't know. You were the one who went after her," she pointed out.

"Well, she ... uh ..." He didn't know how to explain it to

Deedee. Astrid had just disappeared without any explanation or reason. One moment they were talking and then ... *poof*. He'd looked around, checking to see if she was behind him, but there was only empty space.

Where the devil could she have gone to? And more importantly, why?

"Zac," Isabelle whined. "Are we going to the club or not?"

Irritation built up inside of him. Isabelle Anderson hadn't stopped hounding him since last summer when he came to visit. She'd grown up to be a beautiful and confident young woman, but Zac saw her as nothing more than a little sister. An annoying little sister at that, as she tried to insert herself into every outing he had planned with Lucas, Adrianna, or any of their mutual friends.

It was pure coincidence that he'd ordered food at *Petite Louve* tonight and saw Deedee. He couldn't believe Astrid was there too. He hadn't had a chance to go back and observe more of the training since Monday because he'd been busy with work. At least that's what he told himself. Though truth be told, it was also because he had been scared of his reaction to her.

What had been a training and observational exercise for him had turned into something very different. His body's reaction to her had been alarming, and he panicked. But it had also kept him up nights, and he couldn't stop thinking about her. The way she smelled and the feel of her body against him. He wanted to know if her skin felt as soft as it looked or how her naked breasts would feel in his hands. In that brief contact they had, he could have sworn he smelled her arousal.

It had been pure torture, the last few days, but now that she was so close, he didn't want to be away from her. He just wanted one taste, just to see maybe, just maybe, if he did and he felt nothing—or worse, weird—then he could put this damn obsession behind him.

"Zac? Earth to Zac?" Isabelle waved a hand at him, her sparkly bangles jingling as they crashed together. "Well, are we going? My driver's outside waiting."

"What? Oh. No." He shook his head. "I have an early day tomorrow, too."

"But Zac—"

"Goodnight, ladies," he said, ignoring Isabelle's protests. He quickly left the restaurant and made his way back to where he parked his car. He didn't feel guilty at all about leaving suddenly. He wasn't lying after all, as he planned to make a very early day of tomorrow.

———

The next day, Zac headed into the Fenrir Corp.'s headquarters as usual, and walked toward the private elevators. However, instead of going to the executive floor where he had a temporary office set up, he went straight to the fifteenth floor. At this hour, the trainees should still be doing their drills. He had sent a message to his father earlier, letting him know he was going to be stopping by.

"Zac," Nick greeted as he entered the gym. His father

could barely contain the excitement on his face. "I'm glad to see you here."

"Good morning, Dad," he greeted back. "Glad to be here."

"I was hoping you'd come back for another round of observation, you did so well the last time." Nick motioned to follow him.

"I did learn from the best." As head of security for Fenrir, Nick had been well trained in combat and made sure his sons were too. "What's the agenda for today?"

"As you know, mornings are for combat training mostly. Today, we're doing some jujitsu." He pointed to the recruits who were paired off for the sparring sessions.

"Are they—" Zac stopped suddenly when his gaze landed on two of the combatants. Astrid was rolling around the floor with another one of the recruits. One of the male recruits. It looked like she had the advantage, but her partner hooked a leg around her and then landed on top of her.

Zac's inner wolf roared with fury, and his fingers curled into fists, digging into the palms of his hands. Jealousy stabbed at him like a knife to the gut, seeing another man with her. It was irrational and infuriating at the same time, especially since he couldn't do anything about it. It was a training exercise for God's sake, but he still wanted to rip the other man's throat out.

"*Ahem.*" His father's eyes narrowed at him. "Zac, are you all right?"

He tore his gaze away from Astrid and the other man.

"Yes. I'm fine." When he heard Astrid's laugh, his head snapped back. The man was standing now, but he held out his hand to her. She took it and got to her feet, then smiled up at him and spoke in a voice so soft, he couldn't quite hear it. The man's eyes drifted down briefly to the sports bra she wore before looking back up at her pretty face.

Another ugly streak of jealousy speared through him. Did she enjoy having him on top of her? The contact of their bodies? The way the other man's eyes devoured her curves?

"Zac." His father's voice sounded like a warning now. "There's nothing much going on here that you haven't seen before. You should go back to the executive floor. I'm sure Lucas needs you there."

"I'm fine right here," he declared. "I think I really need to know how this training works, especially if I'm to be in charge of the Alpha's security."

Throughout the rest of the morning, Zac remained in the training gym, pretending to listen to his father's and Meredith's instructions or comments, or feigning interest in learning about how the training worked. Like a predator stalking its prey, his gaze fixed on Astrid. If she knew or cared he was here, she didn't show it. It was like she went out of her way to completely ignore him, which only fueled the maelstrom inside him.

Finally, Meredith and Nick declared that the morning session would be over and they could all take their lunch breaks. As the group broke up, Zac tuned his enhanced hearing to eavesdrop on Astrid's conversation.

"You wanna head to the cafeteria, Astrid?" One of the female trainees asked her.

"Sure—oh poop. I left my Fenrir ID back in my room. You know those cafeteria ladies are ruthless when you don't have your card. You guys go ahead and I'll follow." She headed toward the other side of the room, to the stairs that led up to the sixteenth floor barracks.

Before his father could invite him to lunch, he made an excuse about already having plans and quickly left the gym to make sure he was the first one to the executive elevators. Instead of heading back to the lobby, however, he pressed the button for the sixteenth floor.

Swiftly, he darted down the hallway, anticipation pumping in his veins. The door that led to the stairs opened and when he saw the flash of blonde hair, he didn't waste any time. He grabbed Astrid and hauled her through the nearest door he could find—a broom closet, based on the small constrictive space and the various cleaning supplies on the shelves. *Perfect.*

"What in—Zac?" Whisky-colored eyes blinked up at him in surprise. When her gaze darted behind him, he knew he had to act fast.

"Oh, no," he said. "You're not getting away from me again." He pulled on the string hanging from the lone light-bulb above them and plunged the room into darkness.

"What the hell? You can't—mmm—"

Unsure how else to stop her from *poofing* away or protesting, Zac leaned down to press his mouth to hers.

Astrid's lips were velvety soft and warm. She didn't

even protest, but eagerly returned his ardent kiss. Desire surged through him as he slanted his lips and she opened up to him. She tasted like the most delectable dessert in the world. *Mine.* She was all his and he would do his damned best to make her forget about any other man.

She moaned into his mouth and ran her hands up to his shoulders, slipping under his suit jacket. In turn, he moved his hands down her back, cupping her firm ass and pulling her hips to him so she could feel how hard his cock was. She gasped and pressed up against him, grinding herself to his erection, the scent of her arousal filling the tiny space.

He continued his assault on her lips, kissing her senseless, unable to stop. It was like he couldn't get enough of her, feeding a desire inside him that couldn't be quenched. He lifted her up, pinned her against the wall as he wrapped her legs around him, trying to find the perfect angle for her to—

"Oh!" She pulled her lips away from his and threw her head back.

He pressed his lips to her neck and continued to grind his cock against her as he sucked on her soft skin. That delicious scent of hers grew stronger, threatening to overcome him. She raked her fingers through his hair, tugging at the scalp.

"Zac, I—" He smothered her mouth to muffle her scream as her body shook with her orgasm. He kept a grip on his own pleasure, not wanting to come in his pants. No, he wanted to be inside her when that happened. She whimpered and another shudder went through her body before she relaxed against him. He could hear her heartbeat thundering in her chest. Or was that his?

He kissed her temple, feeling the overheated skin. "Astrid, I want—"

"Excuse me, what the hell are you doing in here?"

They both froze at the sound of the unfamiliar voice. The door to the closet had been opened, allowing light to stream in behind the middle-aged woman who stood there, hands on her hips. "You two! No fooling around in my closet. I'm going to report—"

"You will do no such thing," Zac said, his voice taking on a dangerous edge. "Leave," he growled, his wolf coming to the surface. "Now."

The janitor's face grew pale. "I ... uh ..." She shrugged. "I'll be back in fifteen minutes. That better be enough time for you."

When the door slammed shut, the room went dark, but not for long. Light filled the small space and when he turned around, Astrid quickly let go of the string hanging above her. With her hair all disheveled, her skin flushed and lips swollen, all Zac could think of was how sexy she looked and how he wanted to pick up where they'd left off.

"Zac!" she warned, raising her hands up as he took a step forward. "What are you doing?"

"Something you obviously want me to do," he answered, licking his lips.

"I—no!" She stammered. "This can't ... we can't do this."

"Why not?"

"Because ... you know this isn't right." She turned away from him.

"Did I imagine you kissing me back? Or you coming from—"

She shook her head and buried her face in her hands, murmuring something he couldn't understand. "Stop, this is so wrong."

He wanted her to stop saying that. Because none of this felt wrong. "Is it that guy?"

"What guy?"

"The guy that was on top of you." It was hard to say it.

"Guy—oh my God. Joey? We were training, not doing the horizontal mambo," she said. "Besides, what about Isabelle?"

"Who?"

"Isabelle Anderson." The tips of her ears went red.

"Isabelle—Are you jealous of her?"

"No!" she retorted. "I'm not. But I mean, her—she—she's the type of girl you should be with."

"Says who?" he challenged. "She means nothing to me. Astrid, I want *you*. And I know you want me."

"Zac, use your head." She shuffled, moving around him. "Look, you're probably used to girls falling straight into bed with you. I don't know what kind of girl you think I am, but I don't do that."

Now he was confused. "Do what?"

"Just jump into bed with anyone."

"I didn't say that."

"I just ... I know how this works," she said in a quiet voice. "I'm not the kind of ... I mean, we'll have a fun couple of days together, but then you'll go back to London and I have to stay here. And then you'll find someone appropriate for you and I'll just end up ..."

Zac stared at her, stunned. Appropriate? What the hell did that mean?

"Just ... let's not do this, okay? I already know the drill." She reached for the door.

"Wait, Astrid—"

"Don't, Zac. Just don't."

The sound of the door shutting sounded so final to his ears. Like this was it, the end, and that he would never see her again after this.

Perhaps he was going through the stages of *what the fuck just happened* again, but he was sure of one thing: he was not going to accept Astrid's excuses.

CHAPTER EIGHT

strid was glad for the day to be over, at least the first part of it. As soon as the trainees were dismissed, she made a mad dash to her room. She had over an hour to get ready for her shift at The Vixen Den and gobble down dinner somewhere along the way.

Somehow, she made it to the subway, running into the car just as the doors were closing. It was packed, and she found a quiet corner in the back and leaned her head against the wall. This was the first time today she'd even had a chance to think, and the problem with that was once she started, it was like a floodgate opening, and her thoughts came back to that afternoon.

Her mind was still reeling, one moment wondering if that did really happen and that they had kissed, or was it her imagination? Because never in a million years would she thought she would be making out with Zac Vrost.

Well, more than making out. Her body was still buzzing from that orgasm. *Oooh, boy.* The memory of his substantial erection pressed up against her core made her shiver. If things had progressed any further, she was pretty sure she'd be walking funny for two weeks.

It had been too long; dating had never been a priority for her, and save for a few drunken fumbles over the past few years, her sex life was pathetically lacking. Maybe that was the reason she'd thrown herself at him. Maybe she should start putting herself out there again.

Her wolf growled at her, making her startle. *Horny little bitch.* Her animal reveled in Zac's kisses and the way his body felt. Her animal side was partly to blame, as it whined with need when they were interrupted. *Well, too bad.* No way that was happening again. She just couldn't do that to herself. *Not again.*

The PA system called out her stop, and Astrid pushed her way to the front of the car, hopping out and running up the stairs to the street. She ran all the way to the club, which was still two blocks away from the stop. She made it inside, fifteen minutes past the hour she was supposed to have clocked in.

"Yo, girly! Late again. You're fired."

Astrid sighed. Her father told her that the forgetting potion worked as expected, and no one who had witnessed her shifting or using her powers remembered any of it. Maybe she should have asked him to make Mr. G's a little more potent so that he didn't remember all those times she was late. "I'm sorry, Mr. G, I promise—"

"Hey, hey, I was kidding!" Mr. G took his cigar out of his mouth and chuckled. "You think I'm gonna fire one of my best bodyguards? You saved Petal. And besides, the girls would riot if I let you go. I owe ya one. Whatever you need, you ask, okay?"

She breathed a sigh of relief. "Thanks, Mr. G. Actually, would you mind if I bounced a little early tonight? My friend's having this party and—"

"Sure! Just have one of the guys cover the backstage entrance, okay?"

"Thanks, Mr. G, you're the best." Now that she was sure she wasn't going to be fired for being late, she slowed her pace as she made her way to the dressing room. When she entered, she saw most of the girls gathered together, talking quietly.

"Hey, ladies, I'm b Petal?"

The crowd had parted in the middle to allow Astrid to walk over to Petal. When she saw the girl's face—healing, but still bruised, she let out a soft cry. "Oh, Petal, I'm so sorry. This is my fault. I should have—"

"Your fault?" Petal stood up. "None of this is your fault, Astrid. This is all on me for being a damn fool." She embraced Astrid and drew her close. "If anything, I'm still here because of you."

Astrid felt the burn of the tears in her throat. The look of horror on Petal's face that night was still fresh in her mind. Thank goodness she didn't remember a thing. That was the reason Lycans had to conceal their true selves from the humans, but it didn't seem fair. "I let him hurt you," she said. "I should have—"

"Shush." Petal put a finger to Astrid's lips. "Maybe this is what I needed—no, I mean, really. For me to hit rock bottom and finally have the guts to put Leon's sorry ass in jail. I'll be testifying at his trial and making sure he's put away."

"I know a lawyer," Astrid said. "He's my cousin, and he'll help you out. Anthony's the best." She made a mental note to call her cousin, Anthony, in the morning.

"You've done enough, Astrid." Petal assured her. "I can't let you—"

"Don't even think about saying no. I'll take care of it." She frowned. "What are you doing here, by the way? Shouldn't you be at home resting?"

"I can't afford to be out of work," Petal said. "So, Mr. G said if I can come in and keep the dressing rooms tidy, he'll give me a paycheck until I'm ready to come back on stage." She wrinkled her nose. "But, with all these slobs here, I hope I heal sooner rather than later!"

All the girls laughed, and Astrid couldn't help but chuckle too. "That's great, Petal, I'm glad. But if you need anything—"

"Girl, I'm fine." She waved Astrid away. "Go and get to work before Mr. G chews you out again!"

"Yeah, we don't want the man to have an aneurysm or something." She waved to the girls before she headed to her locker to put her stuff away.

Astrid's job was actually pretty boring. Mostly, she

patrolled around the backstage area, checking in with the other security team members. Sometimes, if some very insistent customer tried to sneak in, she would call one of the burly bouncers out front using her walkie-talkie and the customer would be escorted out and banned from ever coming back. Mr. G ran a very tight ship; it was a business, after all, despite whatever went on in the front of the house.

She finished her rounds when she decided to swing by to the dressing rooms for her break. Once again, the girls were gathered together, chatting and gossiping, but this time, they all stopped when Astrid entered.

"Do I have something on my face?" Everyone remained silent. "What's going on?"

"Just tell her, Rose," Coco said.

"What's going on?" Astrid turned to the petite redhead in the leather bustier. "Rose?"

"Well ..." Rose hesitated. "This guy comes in and asks for a lap dance, right? So the boss calls me and I go into the room and he's there. Fancy executive type, dressed in an expensive suit. But before I even start, he stops me, won't even let me near him." She shrugged. "I ask what's his damage, and he says he doesn't want a dance from me, but he gave me a couple hundred to go backstage and deliver a message. To you."

"Me?" Astrid swallowed a gulp. "Who was it?"

"He didn't tell me his name." Rose shrugged her shoulders. "He just said, 'Tell Astrid that fifteen minutes in the closet wouldn't have been enough.'"

That dipstick jacker. What the hell was Zac doing here? "Is he still there?"

"Yeah. Room three."

Her fury barely contained, she made her way to Room three. She threw the door open, and there, sitting on the red velvet couch, was Zac Vrost, looking entirely too pleased with himself when he saw her enter.

"You got my message?"

"Yes. And how. Dare. You!" She stomped over to him. "You can't just come in here!"

"This is a place of business, right?" Zac looked up at her innocently. "And I'm a customer."

"Fine, then I'll call Rose and you can get your lap dance!" She turned to walk away, but Zac used his Lycan speed to get in front of her. "Get out of my way or—"

"Astrid, please."

"Wasn't I clear enough today?"

"Actually, you weren't." He straightened his shoulders. "Those things you said about not doing this to each other and knowing the drill didn't make any sense. We're adults, we can do what we want."

Oh, why was he making this difficult? It was embarrassing enough as it is. She didn't want to think about the past and what they were. "Zac, you and I move in different circles. You're the Beta's son, not to mention, your dad's like a bajillionaire and your mom's Cady Vrost, the most classy woman on the planet. You went to Harvard, then Oxford, and now you help run this huge company, not to mention, you'll probably soon be second-in-command of the largest Lycan clan in the world."

"So?"

"So? I'm just a fuckup nobody. I dropped out of college after one semester, and I've been drifting from job to job, year after year, pretending I'm an adult." Reliving how much of a failure she was wasn't really helping her confidence, but she was trying to make a point. "I finally find a job I like and I fuck that up too, and nearly expose our kind to the humans. I'm just no good for you, Zac."

His expression turned dark. "First of all, you're not a fuckup and if you say anything like that again, I swear I'm going to put you over my knee and spank you. Your parents are respected in the Lycan community, but even if they weren't, I don't give a shit about that. Second, it's not like I'm asking you to marry me."

She tried to ignore the sting of those words. "If you want a quick fuck, I told you, I'm not that kind of girl."

"For God's sake, Astrid." He rubbed his palm down his face. "That's not what I want."

"Then what do you want?" She was getting frustrated. "Why did you kiss me?"

"I don't know ... I just ... I had to."

"Had to?"

"Well, why did you kiss me back?" he countered.

She didn't have a comeback for that one. "Zac, I'm tired of going in circles with you. What will it take to make you go away?"

He was silent for a moment. "Kiss me again and then tell me you don't want me."

"Fine." She reached up and pulled him down to give him a quick smack on the lips. "Now go."

His eyes darkened. "You didn't say you didn't want me. And that's not the kind of kiss I meant."

Before she could protest, he wrapped his arms around her and pulled her against him. Shock ran down her spine as his lips landed on hers in a fierce kiss. Her knees immediately went weak, and she lost all will to fight him off, despite the ringing alarm bells in her head. A hand moved up her ribcage to cup her breast, and she moaned into his mouth. She had no choice but to cling to him, as she surely would have melted into a puddle by now.

Zac maneuvered her around and walked her back against the wall, trapping her. Escape was the farthest thing from her mind, especially when all the pleasure centers in her brain seemed to have lit up like Christmas lights. She moved her hands down, feeling his hardened cock through his jeans, and this time it was his turn to moan and thrust his hips against her hand.

"What the fuck is going on here?"

Mr. G's furious voice was like getting doused with a bucket of ice water, and Astrid quickly pushed Zac away. "I'm sorry! Shit, I'm—"

"You!" Mr. G pointed a meaty finger at Zac's face. "She's not one of the dancers. I sent you Rose. What the hell happened to her?"

"I can explain," Astrid began. "I—"

"I'm sorry, Mr. Garavaggio." Zac's voice was cool and collected. He didn't even flinch at Mr. G.'s accusatory glare. "It's all my fault, I'm afraid."

"You can't be touching none of my staff, whether they're dancers or part of the crew. We got rules here."

"I know, sir. Again, my apologies for the misunderstanding. I thought Astrid had told you about me."

"Oh, yeah?" Mr. G chomped on his cigar. "Who the hell are you?"

"I'm Astrid's boyfriend. Zac Vrost." He held his hand out.

"What?" *Oh God, this is what going crazy felt like.*

"Boyfriend, huh?" Mr. G looked Zac up and down.

"Yes, sir. It's our anniversary tonight," Zac explained. "But you know, Astrid's such a hard worker and really cares so much about your girls, she didn't want to take the night off. Especially after what happened last week. Poor girl, that Petal."

Mr. G eyed Astrid. "Girly, if you wanted the night off, ya could have said so, instead of asking to bounce early."

"Er, well. See, I didn't need—"

"All right, all right, you twisted my arm." Mr. G waved his hands dramatically. "Go on, girly, get your things and go have fun with your man."

"But, Mr. G—"

"Ah, stop or you'll give me *agita*! I ain't letting you spend your anniversary with your handsome boyfriend here in the lap dance room," the old man exclaimed. "Now go before I change my mind. Sheesh!" He shook his head as he pivoted on his heel. "Whaddaya got to do to give someone a night off around here?"

As soon as the door shut, Astrid's gaze narrowed at Zac. "You did not just do that!"

"What?" he asked innocently. "Get you the night off?"

"No! Call yourself my ... my ..."

"Boyfriend? It got you out of trouble, right?"

"It got *you* out of trouble, mister!" She poked at his chest for emphasis, but he caught her hand. She ignored the sparks of electricity the contact of his skin sent along her fingers.

"Seeing as you are now free and clear, shall we head over to Blood Moon? Deedee's waiting."

"I'm not going." She pulled her hand back and put her hands on her hips.

"Deedee's your best friend," Zac pointed out. "She'd be crushed if you didn't show up tonight."

"I—" She let out a frustrated sound. Deedee would never forgive her if she didn't show up, plus she'd have to explain. "Fine. But I'm not going with you." She ran out of the room before he could protest.

————

After gathering her things and changing out of her work clothes, Astrid left the building through the employee's entrance in the back, hoping to avoid Zac altogether. She thought she was home free, but when she got to the end of the rear alley, a sleek black Porsche blocked her way.

The door swung open. "Get in," Zac said from the driver's side.

She narrowed her eyes at him. "If this is you trying to show me I'm wrong about how different we are, I'm afraid it's having the exact opposite effect."

"I know," he said in an uncharacteristically cheerful manner. "Are you getting in or not?"

Astrid had two choices: slide over the hood of the sports car and escape or get in. "Fine." She slid inside the car. "Oh God, these seats are amazing," she sighed. They were buttery soft and luxurious.

"They're heated, too." He turned a dial on the dash.

She sank into the seat. "*Oohhhh.* I could live right here." She gave him a smirk. "So, Mr. Vrost, is this how you get unsuspecting women into your car?"

"Only you, Ms. Jonasson," he said with a devilish smile before turning his gaze back on the road. He had his sleeves rolled up to his elbows, the muscles of his tattooed forearm flexing as he put the car into gear.

Astrid groaned inwardly. *Jesus H. Christ,* did everything the man do have to turn her on? Everything about Zac reminded her of this car—it screamed sex and was totally unattainable to her. Why she even let him manipulate her into this situation, she didn't know. It was like all she had to do was smell his incredible scent and look into those sexy ice blue eyes, and she would do anything he wanted. Just the thought of him dominating her—

"Penny for your thoughts?" he said.

"I'm sure you could afford more." She crossed her arms

and turned away from him, instead, focusing her attention on the road.

In his sleek little car, they made it to their destination in no time. Blood Moon was a night club in midtown Manhattan, one that catered to Lycans and magical people. It was partly owned by the Alpha himself, and while they weren't allowed to shift inside the club, many Lycans went there to mingle and socialize with their kind. Zac stopped the car in front of the entrance.

"Parking's a bitch in midtown, so I guess I'll see you later." *Or never*. Astrid unbuckled her seatbelt. "Thanks for the ride."

"They have valet—"

She didn't let him finish, but instead hopped out of the car and dashed straight to the club entrance. She hastily gave the hostess her name, and as soon as she crossed the velvet ropes, headed straight for the doors that led to The Lounge in the back of the building.

Blood Moon's ultra-plush VIP room was closed off from the main section of the club, and as the name implied, was a secret lounge area for the club's most important guests. It was more calm inside, which was probably why Deedee decided to have her party here, despite hating night clubs. As she crossed the room, she said hello to a few people she recognized, but kept craning her neck, trying to look for Deedee. Finally, she spotted the guest of honor coming out of the bathrooms.

"I need a drink." She grabbed her best friend's arm and

dragged her over to the bar. "Dirty martini," she said to the bartender. "Extra martini. Extra olives. Extra alcohol."

"What in the world—I thought you weren't coming until later," Deedee said.

"I thought so too. But I got the night off." She trained her eyes on the bartender, watching as he prepared her drink. It barely landed on the bar before she picked it up and knocked it back.

"Then why are you drinking like your puppy died? Oh my God, Astrid, did you get fired again?"

"I'll have you know, I only get fired from my jobs about 47 percent of the time." She pushed the empty glass toward the bartender. "One more, please. And one for my friend. Thanks."

"What in the world is going on then?" Deedee asked. "Are you upset about last night still?"

"Last night?" She wrinkled her brows together.

"You know. Isabelle."

"Oh, *her*." She'd actually forgotten about Isabelle.

"In case you were looking for the lovely Miss Anderson," Deedee began, "her invitation might have gotten lost in the mail."

Astrid's jaw dropped. "You didn't."

Deedee feigned a sigh. "Oh, technology these days. Text messages could easily get lost in cyberspace."

"You sneaky bitch."

"Meh, I never liked her." Deedee smirked. "Do you know when I told her I was going to school for archeology, she asked me if a Sagittarius would make a good boyfriend for a Leo?"

Astrid howled in laughter. "She *didn't*."

"Oh, yeah."

"What did you say?"

"Well, I—"

"Hello ladies."

Crap.

Zac sidled up to them. "Congratulations, Deedee." He leaned down and pressed a kiss to her cheek.

"Thanks, Zac," Deedee replied. "What are you doing here? I thought you said you couldn't make it?"

"Wait, you weren't even planning to be here?" Astrid asked, her voice rising.

"What can I say? You convinced me to come." Zac's gaze became heavy-lidded. "Plus, I know you enjoyed that ride I gave you."

Heat crept up her cheeks and she knew he wasn't talking about the Porsche. "I did not—"

"Zac!" Lucas grabbed his friend's shoulder. "You made it. I told Adrianna you wouldn't show up. C'mon!"

"I—" Zac tried to protest, but Lucas tugged him toward one of the couches where Adrianna and a few of their cousins and friends were waiting.

Astrid breathed a sigh of relief when Zac let Lucas drag him away.

"You convinced Zac to come?" Deedee raised a delicate brow at her. "Something you want to tell me?"

"It's not what you think."

"Somehow, I doubt it." She grabbed her hand. "What's going on with you and Zac? When you left last night, he tore after you like his life depended on it. Then, he came back inside, looking for you."

"I don't—"

"Spill, Miz Jonasson," Deedee demanded.

"*Fiddlefucker.*" She took the two drinks the bartender put in front of them and gulped both down. "Zac and I ... he kissed me."

"He *what?*" Deedee looked at her in disbelief. "Where? When? How?"

"In the closet. This afternoon. With, er, his mouth?"

"Oh. My. Freaking. *God.*" Her eyes went wide. "You and Zac made—"

"Shush!" She covered Deedee's mouth with her palm. "If I tell you the whole story, do you promise to keep your voice down?" The other girl nodded. "All right." She took her hand away and proceeded to tell Dee the story about the broom closet and the private room at The Vixen Den.

"Holy Moly." Deedee's mouth was formed into a perfect O. "What are you going to do now?"

"I don't know." Astrid buried her face in her hands. "Avoid Zac for the next year or so?"

"Fat chance," Deedee snorted. "While he may have this cool exterior, I know that when Zac wants something, he's like a rabid dog. He's not going to just let this go."

"Then what should I do?"

"Don't you like him back? Why did you make out with him twice today then?"

"I told you why. It's just ... he's him and I'm me." She chewed on her lip. "It's just ... impossible you know. Could you imagine what Cady Vrost would think? Her golden boy and me? Plus, Nick would shit a brick."

"What? Cady and Nick are the nicest people in the world," Deedee said. "Why would they think bad of you?"

"Well, you know ..."

"I don't." Deedee crossed her arms over her chest. "You're my best friend and I think you're fabulous."

Astrid gave her a weak smile. "Thanks. But we're just from different worlds. And he's way out of my league."

"How very classist of you," Dee snorted. "What are we —in the dark ages? Do you need to seek Nick Vrost's approval for his son's hand in marriage? Will you be bringing an appropriate dowry?"

"You don't understand." Of course she didn't; being older than her and with her father's close ties to the Alpha, plus being the daughter of the only billionaire dragon shifter in the world, Deedee had a certain standing in the community, just like Zac.

Astrid's parents, on the other hand, didn't hold any type of honor or title in the Lycan community. Her mother was basically Nick's assistant and her father ... well, she didn't know what Daric did exactly, except that the Alpha would often send him away on errands.

"So, you don't like him and you don't want to be with him?" Deedee asked. "If that's the case, then that's different. Just tell him you don't want him."

For the second time that night, she couldn't deny that she wanted him. She wanted to say it, but the words just wouldn't form in her mouth. "I ... look, I should get some fresh air."

"Astrid—"

"You should see to your other guests." She motioned to the group of people coming in. "I'll be fine, I'll chat with you later okay?" She walked away from the bar and headed out toward the stairwell that led to the rooftop deck. Since it was still wintertime, the area was closed, but she ignored the sign and went out anyway.

It was cold outside, even for a Lycan, and the wind made the temperature drop even further. She shivered visibly, mist forming in front of her when she breathed. She walked to the edge and peered down, watching the street below.

"What are you doing out here by yourself?"

Astrid froze, recognizing the voice. She whipped around and stood there, stunned, not sure if she was seeing things. "Cross?"

Her brother stood there, his face clear in the moonlight. "Hello, Astrid."

"Cross!" she flung herself into his arms. She bit the inside of her cheek, trying not to cry. "I've missed you."

His strong arms wrapped around her. "I've missed you too, Astrid." When she pulled away, he looked down at her with those blue-green eyes which reminded her so much of her dad. "Why are you crying?"

She wiped the tears from her cheeks. "It's nothing. I

mean, I'm just happy to see you. You've been away for months, and Dad won't tell anyone where you've gone."

"I'm sorry, Astrid," he sighed. "It's ... I'm doing some important work."

"Then why won't Mom or Dad say anything?"

"It's for your protection," he said. "For everyone's protection."

"What are you doing here, then?" she asked. "Why show up now?"

He brushed away the remaining wetness on her cheeks. "I've finished part of my work. Plus, you know how insistent Deedee can get."

Astrid chuckled. "Yes, I do." She sucked in a breath. "You came back for her?"

"It's not what you think," Cross said. "I am back for many reasons."

"But—"

"You're cold," he said suddenly. With a wave of his hand, a fur-lined cloak appeared around her shoulders.

"Oohhh." She wrapped the cloak more firmly around her. "Thanks." Like her, Cross had inherited some of their father's powers. But, while she only got a portion of Daric's magic, Cross received a majority of them, including the power of transmogrification, or changing the form of matter. It was one of the more difficult types of magic to master, as it required a lot of knowledge of materials and practice.

"Is that better?" he asked.

"Yes." She hugged him again, smelling his familiar,

comforting scent. "Well, I don't care why you're back. I'm just glad you are. And—"

"*Get away from her.*"

Both she and Cross went rigid.

"She's *mine*," Zac growled. "And I won't let you—Cross?"

Her brother released her and turned around. "Zachary." He stretched out to his full height, which was a good three or four inches more than Zac.

"Cross? Where did you come from? I didn't see anyone come up here except Astrid," Zac said.

"I was invited to this party," he said. "And what do you mean when you said my sister was *yours?*"

Astrid could feel both their wolves now, snarling and staring each other down. "Cross, stop," she said, tugging at her brother's arm. "Please. We should go back and—"

The sound of an explosion cut her off and made all three of them stop dead. An ice-cold feeling gripped her, and it wasn't the sub-zero temps. "The Lounge."

Zac's face darkened. "Astrid, stay here." He looked at Cross, who nodded and grabbed Zac by the shoulders.

"Motherfu—No!" She reached out to grab onto her brother, but it was too late. They were gone. "Stupid, Cross!" Her brother had also inherited Daric's ability to cross long distances and bring people along.

Well, if they think I'm going to stay here, then they're both stupid.

CHAPTER NINE

Zac felt the coldness grip him as Cross' magic surrounded his body. He had a feeling that the hybrid had the same power as his father, if only evidenced by the fact that he had appeared on the rooftop without Zac seeing him. He was with Lucas, Adrianna, and their other friends when he saw Astrid head toward the rooftop. After making excuses to the table, he went after her.

Seeing her in the arms of another man drove him and his wolf insane. He wanted to tear that man's heart out. To say that he was shocked when he realized it was her brother would be an understatement, though it did not mollify his wolf. Cross' wolf was no more dominant than his, and it was not going to cower to anyone. But then that explosion from below had his blood growing cold in his veins.

The coldness left, and Zac felt the ground underneath

his feet. Cross had transported them into the men's bathrooms. He didn't bother waiting for the other man as he darted out to the main lounge.

The scene outside was chaotic. Screams and growls. People running away. Broken glass and furniture. *What the hell was going on?* There were at least a dozen robed figures scattered about the room, waving their hands and throwing bottles on the floor that blew up into smoke. *Magic potions.* Were they being attacked by witches?

"No!"

Zac turned his head toward the scream. Two of the men in robes had grabbed Adrianna, holding her down as a third man threw a small vial at her. She had been screaming and fighting, her body in the middle of a shift as fur sprouted all over her skin. When the green smoke blew up around her, she went limp and the two men lifted her up.

"Adrianna!" Lucas screamed from across the room. Two men in robes blocked him, their hands raised.

Zac felt the blood drain from his face. "Stop him!" He looked around. He recognized several friends in Lycan form fighting off the attackers. Cross was there too, waving his hand and sending three men slamming into the wall. "Cross!" he called to the other man. "Get Adrianna! Now!"

Cross looked at him, and his gaze went toward the men who were dragging Adrianna away. "I'll grab her. Don't let him shift!" Cross disappeared as he left his warning.

Zac didn't know how Cross knew, but there wasn't any

time for that. He was the closest to Lucas, and thus the only one who could help.

"Lucas, no!" He leapt forward, quickly changing into his Lycan form, his clothes ripping away like paper. He landed on all fours and ran to Lucas. The two robed men were holding him down. This was not good.

A loud roar reverberated through the air and the shockwave of power rippling across the room nearly knocked Zac's wolf off its paws. His animal shrank back instinctively, but Zac fought it and urged it to go forward. *We have to get to him*, he told his wolf. *Help him. Save him. From himself.* Because he knew for certain that Lucas would not be the one who needed saving.

Fuck!

Lucas had fully turned into his Lycan form, a wolf that was so dominant and terrifying that all the Lycans in the room were surely paralyzed with fear. The wolf was pure black and was over eight feet on its hind legs, its massive jaw ripping and snarling at the two attackers. In a blur of dark fur, both men were underneath its gigantic paws, and his fearful, gaping maw came down with a vicious snarl.

Zac pushed his wolf forward, fighting its instinct to lay down and show its belly. Lucas was not in control in this state, not when Adrianna was in danger. He had to somehow reach Lucas inside his wolf. And he couldn't do it like this.

"Lucas!" he called when he shifted back to his human form. He changed back too quickly, and he felt dizzy, but he had to keep going. "Lucas, they're dead. Stop."

The wolf raised its head from the carnage, blood dripping from its snout. Blue-green eyes glowed in the dim light, and Zac felt the hairs on his arms rise. There was no recognition in his eyes, only pure animal violence. Lucas had shifted and gone straight into bloodlust.

This had only happened twice before, and no one—not Grant, Frankie, his father, or any Lycan doctor—could say why Lucas' wolf had acted this way. Shifting in bloodlust wasn't like going feral. Every other time he shifted, he was in control. Perhaps being the son of two Alphas made his wolf extremely dominant and powerful, but why he went out of control, no one could say for certain.

"*Lucas,*" he emphasized. "Please, change back."

The wolf growled at him and snapped its jaw, then began to stalk toward him.

"Cross is here, Lucas. He's going to save Adrianna." He kept repeating his name, hoping he would remember who he was. "Don't do this, Lucas." He knew this would rip his friend apart, knowing that he killed those men. "Lucas!"

The wolf leapt at him, and he braced himself, ready to shift and tangle with Lucas if only to slow him down and stop him from hurting anyone else. But the wolf never came. A white blur whizzed past his eyes, knocking the Alpha wolf down.

"No!" He knew that scent. And he knew in his bones who it was. "Astrid, no!" He forced the shift as quickly as he could; it was painful as this was his second shift in minutes, but he had no choice. His heart banged into his ribcage, and he prayed it wouldn't be too late as he vaulted toward where Astrid and Lucas were tangled in a flurry of black and white fur.

Lucas was much bigger than Astrid's wolf, so he quickly gained the upper hand. She howled in pain as his paw swiped at her. Rage poured in his veins, and Zac sprang forward.

"Lucas! Stop!"

Zac's wolf skidded to a halt when he heard Adrianna's pleading cries. She hobbled over to Lucas, unafraid of the wolf. Her hair was disheveled and one of her shoes were gone, but she seemed unharmed otherwise. She embraced the wolf, whispering soothing words. This was the only way to get Lucas under control when he was in bloodlust.

Zac breathed a sigh of relief and padded over to Astrid. Thank God she was unhurt. He leaned down and sniffed at her, pressing his muzzle to her neck, breathing in that heady, flowery scent. The white wolf whined and licked at his face.

"Everything seems to be under control." Cross had reappeared beside them. "All of the Lycans are safe, save for a few injuries. But our attackers got away."

Zac stepped away from Astrid to give her some space as she began to shift back. He turned away and did the same, pushing his wolf deep inside him, taking control of their body once again as he changed back into his human form. With a pained grunt, he got up from his knees. "Thanks," he grumbled to Cross as, with a wave of his hand, his clothes reappeared on his body. It was the first time he'd seen this particular power and it unnerved him.

"Cross! Is she okay?" Astrid too had changed back and was also fully clothed.

"What the hell were you thinking?" Zac bit out, grabbing her by the shoulders. "Do you have any idea ... you could have been killed!"

"What the hell was I supposed to do?" she retorted. "He was coming after you and you were standing there like a deer in headlights. Were you just going to let him hurt you?"

"I had to!" He gripped her shoulders harder.

"If he had ... and you were ..." Her face went pale. "I don't understand. Who were those people? And Lucas ... what's wrong with him?"

"Nothing," he said defensively. "It's not my story to tell." Adrenaline was slowly draining out of him, and he stumbled forward. Astrid caught him and wrapped her arms around his torso. He breathed in her scent, letting it wrap around and consume him. "Astrid," he said in a broken voice, his hand coming up to her back. He genuinely thought Lucas would kill her. He'd seen it in Lucas' eyes. He had been close, the bloodlust fueling his rage. If something happened to her—

Cross clearing his throat made them disentangle from each other. "I think it's time we called the Alpha." He looked at Astrid. "Mom and Dad are—"

"Here," Daric announced as he materialized behind them. He slipped his hand from Meredith's waist. He looked around. The Lounge had been thoroughly trashed by their attackers and the Lycans who had shifted to protect themselves. Broken pieces of the fashionable and ultra-modern furniture lay scattered on the ground. The glittering chandelier that was the centerpiece of the room was shattered into a million pieces. Tables were overturned and spilled bottles of alcohol were everywhere.

"Let's get to work," he said. "I'll see to anyone who has any injuries. I've brought a few potions and antidotes just in case. Cross?"

"I'll head out," he said, "and see what evidence they left behind."

"Astrid, a little help?" Meredith said to her daughter. "We should secure the area."

Astrid nodded. "All right."

Zac was reluctant to see Astrid go, but for now, she was safe. "What can I do?"

Daric placed a hand on his shoulder. "Your mother and father are stuck in traffic, so perhaps you can keep the authorities busy? I suspect we will get a visit from the NYPD."

He nodded. "Will do."

Zac headed outside to the main club area to assess any further damage. He met with the manager, a Lycan named Sean Presley. The club had to be shut down as someone—probably a bystander outside or one of the stray humans who somehow ventured into the club—called 911. Since Zac would be facing the police, they came up with a story that could be easily verified later—that Zac was a silent partner in the club, as well as a guest at the party.

The beat cops who arrived were easy enough to placate. Zac explained that there had been a fight inside between two of the patrons. "One of them was hitting on the other guy's girlfriend," he explained to a uniformed officer. "You know how that is, sir."

The man interviewing Zac flipped his notebook closed. "Yeah, unfortunately. But we should really investigate and talk to more people."

"Would that really be worth your time, Officer Martinez? Aren't there more serious crimes going on outside?"

"I suppose." He put his notebook away. "Are you pressing charges, Mr. Vrost?"

"Oh, no," he chuckled. "If we had to press charges against every jealous boyfriend or girlfriend who cause trouble around here, we'd be up to our necks in lawsuits, you know what I mean?"

"Yeah. Too bad those two guys got away, huh?"

"Too bad. Well now, I guess—"

"Excuse me."

Officer Martinez' face turned sour before he turned around. "Well, hello, Detective." He did not sound happy.

The dark-haired woman who interrupted them nodded at Martinez, her face blank. "Officer." She turned to Zac. "I'm Detective Sofia Selinofoto." She held up a badge. "And you are?"

"Zac Vrost," he said, offering a hand. "I'm one of the partners here."

Selinofoto ignored his hand. "So, can you tell me what happened?"

"I've already given my statement to the officer."

She gave him a freezing look with her steely light gray eyes. "Then you can give it to me again."

If he were a lesser man, he would have been intimidated. Still, she was an officer of the law. Besides, the New York clan was well connected in the city. One call to the police chief and this would all go away. For now, he would cooperate. "Fine," he said. "I was inside The Lounge when—shit!"

"Shit?" Selinofoto raised a dark brow.

"That's not, I mean—excuse me." He sidestepped around the detective, heading toward the private doors. Zac cursed again, this time, to himself. Lucas, dressed only in his pants, had somehow stumbled out of The Lounge. Last he had seen his friend, he was out cold on one of the benches as the shift had wiped him out. *How the hell did he get out?* "Lucas," he hissed. "You're not doing too good." Zac slipped an arm around his chest to steady him.

"Zac," he mumbled. "I—" When he lifted his face up, his expression sobered and his pupils dilated. "Who are—"

"Mr. Vrost." Selinofoto's cool voice cut Lucas off. "What's going on?" The door to The Lounge was ajar and she peeked inside. "What the hell happened in there?"

Zac cursed silently and he used his foot to kick the door shut and then swung Lucas around to his other arm.

"Nothing, Detective," he said quickly. "Just … a private party."

"You're still having a party in there? After what happened?"

"Well, business is business. You know how cutthroat rent is in Manhattan. I can't afford to shut down."

Her gaze turned to Lucas, and for a moment, her eyes glazed over. She shook her head and her dark brows furrowed together. "What's wrong with him?"

"Just a little too much to drink. It's his, er, bachelor party," he said. "You know how it is. Last days of freedom."

She looked taken aback, then her expression turned cold again. "Well, then, why don't you send the groom back to the party and come and make your statement."

"No …" Lucas slurred. "You—"

"Will do, Detective. Come along now, all your friends are waiting." Zac opened the door and dragged Lucas inside. "Adrianna," he called.

"Zac!" She went over to him and put her arms around Lucas. "I just went to the bathroom and he was gone."

"It's okay," Zac said. "I caught him before he went too far."

"I'll take care of him," she said, leading her brother toward one of the couches in the corner.

God, this night was turning into a shit show. How did his parents do this? "Daric," he called to the warlock who was chatting softly with his wife.

"Zachary," he greeted. "Is everything all right?"

"There's a detective from the NYPD in the main room.

She may have gotten a glimpse in here, and she definitely saw Lucas. I think she'll need a dose of that forgetting potion."

"I'll administer it then." He took a vial from the pouch slung over his shoulder. "Is she right outside?"

"Yes. Detective Sofia Selinofoto. She's about five feet, five inches tall with dark hair, wearing a navy blouse, and slacks."

Daric nodded before he headed for the door. Zac turned to Meredith. "Everything okay in here?"

"Yeah," she answered. "Grant and Frankie are five minutes away, and Nick and Cady just got here. How is he?"

Zac looked back at Lucas who was still on the couch. "He'll be okay." *I hope.*

The last time Lucas had shifted in bloodlust had not been pretty. He should know; he'd been there to witness it. But Lucas supposedly had it under control, and even spent an entire year in a special program with another clan to learn to placate the bloodlust. Zac couldn't blame him, however. Seeing his twin being taken away had probably brought up bad memories.

"We'll stay here until the police are gone," Meredith said. "Hopefully, there'll be no press, but if I know your mother, she's already working her magic."

"And if Daric works his magic, we won't have to worry about that detective." There was something about Selinofoto that he just couldn't put his finger on. Something in her expression that said she didn't believe there was nothing fishy going on. He glanced around. "Where's Astrid ... and Cross?" he added quickly.

"They're around somewhere," Meredith said. "I think Cross went out to investigate and find any clues about those guys that attacked."

"Do you have any idea what they were after? Or who they were?"

Meredith had a look on her face he had never seen before—worry. "We do. But we should wait until everyone gets here."

———

Once the police were gone and the press thoroughly placated, everyone gathered back in The Lounge. Aside from those who were already at the party, Grant, Frankie, Nick, Cady, and much to Zac's surprise, a few other people he didn't expect had arrived as well. Grant's sister, Alynna and her husband Alex were there, as well as Sebastian Creed and his mate Jade, and the men who headed Lone Wolf Security—Killian Jones, Quinn Martin, and the feral wolf himself, Connor Forrest. The latter three, if Zac remembered clearly, were also adoptive brothers to Meredith, and thus, Astrid's uncles.

"Something tells me there's more to this than just a kidnapping attempt," Sebastian Creed began, his gray eyes going steely.

"I'm afraid so," Grant said. "Daric?"

The warlock stepped forward, his expression grave.

"Our enemies are back."

"Enemies?" Killian asked. "You mean—"

"The mages."

A dead silence filled the air. Zac knew all about the mages. Thirty years ago, right around the time he was born, an evil master mage named Stefan had sought to kill all the Lycans in the world. Mages were former witches or warlocks who used blood magic to increase their power, a forbidden type of magic that relied on killing people, and thus, breaking the laws of nature.

"But we got rid of them," Sebastian said. "We killed every single last one of them. I burned that motherfucker Stefan myself." He turned to Daric. "Did he survive? What do you know? How long have you known?"

"I've suspected for some time now," Daric confessed. "I told the Alpha, but I wasn't sure. I needed to investigate, but if any of the former mages in Stefan's coven did survive, they would have known me instantly. I had to send someone to find out more."

"That's why you've been gone," Astrid said to Cross. "Dad sent you away, didn't he? To investigate."

Cross nodded. "Yes."

"What did you discover?" Grant asked.

"I've not quite completed my investigation," Cross said. "New mages are on the rise, though they still conceal their presence. But I have seen it with my own eyes."

"Motherfuckers," Alynna cursed. "Well, we'll kick their asses again and again. They're not going to get rid of us easily."

"I don't understand," Lucas said. He had fully regained his strength and was sitting beside his twin. "Why attack now? And why did they try to kidnap Adrianna?"

"I'm not sure," Cross said. "But they weren't just trying to kidnap Adrianna. They were trying to capture you too."

"Me?"

"I believe they are trying to stop you both from ascending to Alpha." Cross's face drew into a grim expression.

"They tried to kidnap and kill me once too," Grant said.

"What should we do, then?" Killian asked.

"Well, this time, they won't catch us by surprise," Nick said. "Now that we know they're after us, we can prepare ourselves."

"And possibly strike first," Sebastian added, his steely eyes turning golden, signaling the presence of his dragon.

"We'll do that and more," Frankie said. "First, we need to ramp-up security on Adrianna and Lucas, maybe Julianna and Isabelle too."

"What? I haven't had a protective detail since I was eighteen when Shane retired," Adrianna said, referring to their former manny–bodyguard.

"You should really have someone from the security team with you at all times," Grant said. "You're not just my daughter, but a future Alpha yourself."

"I told you, that's unnecessary," Adrianna huffed. "And you all are being ridiculous."

"I think it's a great idea," Lucas said. "You know I've never supported dropping your security detail."

"I don't like it," she said sourly.

"Please, *mimma*," Frankie soothed, placing a hand on her daughter's shoulder. "You'll need it. The mages obviously have something planned for you both, and we need to make sure they don't succeed. You have no idea what they're capable of and the lengths they'll go to."

"There may be something bigger at play here, Adrianna," Alynna said thoughtfully. "A reason why they don't want you two to become Alphas."

"Nick," Grant began. "Do we have enough people to cover my kids?"

"It'll be tight," Nick said. "But I can make it work. Maybe Adrianna can stay close to Fenrir or stay in The Enclave until I can figure something out."

"I can't stay at home. They need me at work." Adrianna was president of Muccino International, the restaurant chain her mother's family owned. "And we have that big conference in Vail. We're supposed to leave the day after tomorrow, Lucas."

"We should cancel the trip." Lucas's whole body stiffened. "You'll be safer in New York, at home. I'm not letting anyone get to you again."

Her face softened. "The mages won't get to me. No one will."

"We won't let anything happen to her," Nick promised. "But having both of you together makes you a tempting target. That's probably why they struck tonight."

"Two birds with one stone," Alynna said. "It would be harder for them to kidnap you if you were separated for now."

"I suppose that makes sense," Lucas relented. "But can I make a suggestion regarding Adrianna's security detail?"

"Of course," Nick said.

"Aside from whomever you're assigning to her, I want an additional person with her at all times."

"Who?" Nick asked.

"Astrid."

All eyes turned to the blonde Lycan. Zac, on the other hand, shot his friend a curious look.

"Me?" Astrid said.

"Yes," Lucas said. "She's the obvious choice, isn't she? As a girl, she'll be able to stick to Adrianna everywhere."

"I'll definitely be more comfortable with someone I know," Adrianna added.

"But she's not even a part of the security team," Nick said. "She's only a trainee."

Zac had his reservations as well, mainly because he didn't want Astrid in harm's way. But before he could say anything, Daric spoke up.

"Astrid has not been involved in Lycan or magical affairs in any way," he began. "And she and I have made sure no one knows of her abilities. I think she will make a great asset."

"And she's running circles around the other trainees," Meredith added, the pride in her tone evident. "She's been trained since she was seven. And by the best." She glanced over at Connor who remained stony, though his shoulders seemed to straighten with pride.

Nick look perturbed, but shrugged. "Astrid? Do you agree?"

She glanced at Meredith, who gave her the thumbs-up sign. "Yes, of course. My parents fought the mages, and I'll do my part as well."

"It's settled then," Grant said. "Astrid will travel with Adrianna to Colorado. Starting tomorrow though, you should stick to her. We can say you're her personal assistant. Now, as for the mages, I think we all need time to digest the information, plus Cross will be giving me a full report on what he's discovered. I'll summon you all for a meeting once we've finished his debriefing."

"We'll get those bastards before they can come after any of us." Sebastian glanced at his mate and daughter. "And when we find them, I'm going to burn those mother-fuckers twice over to make sure they're dead."

"Get some rest," Frankie said. "And please, be vigilant, and don't take any unnecessary risks."

A few of them stayed to get more details, but mostly, everyone began to file out of the room. Zac made a beeline for Lucas, who finished saying goodbye to his parents.

"Why her?" Zac said.

"What?" He looked confused.

"Astrid. Why did you volunteer her?" He kept his hands fisted at his sides. Lucas was a friend, but if anything happened to Astrid …

"Look, you know how stubborn Adrianna is. She

would never agree to a security detail unless it was someone she knew." His eyes went steely. "And I would do anything to protect her."

But at what cost? Zac gritted his teeth to stop himself from saying the words out loud. "Lucas, I know she's your sister, but you can't let what happened in the past—"

"Stop." Lucas' voice was deadly calm. "I don't want to talk about the past."

"Are you sure you can control yourself?" Zac pivoted. "The bloodlust—"

"And that's why I want her protected." Lucas cocked his head. "Is there any reason you're objecting to having Astrid guard my sister?"

"Of course not," he said quickly. "But she's not one of the security team."

"You sound like your father," he pointed out.

"Astrid attacked you," Zac shot back.

"Exactly." He cleared his throat. "I know you're confused. What I'm trying to say is, despite her wolf's natural instinct to run away from me, she charged at me anyway. And that's why I know she'll do her best to protect Adrianna. I just ... have this gut feeling, okay?"

Zac's shoulders sagged in defeat. "You'll be Alpha soon, so I have no choice but to trust your decision." He knew the threat of the mages was serious. But, that's why he was worried. If anything happened to Astrid ... his chest tightened at the thought. He had to do something. Because just like Lucas would do anything to protect his twin, he would do the same for Astrid.

CHAPTER TEN

As Astrid sat in the plush chair inside the Muccino International private jet as it sat on the tarmac, she started to forget why she even had second thoughts of taking this job.

"Thanks, Steve," she said to the handsome flight steward who refilled her champagne glass.

"My pleasure, Ms. Jonasson." He tipped up the bottle. "Anything else I can get for you before we take off?"

"Hmm ..." She took a sip of her champagne. "How about more of those salmon thingies? And some chocolate truffles?"

"Of course, Ms. Jonasson." As he turned around and walked back toward the galley, Astrid couldn't help but stare at the way his ass filled in those tight, white uniform pants. *I could get used to living like this.* She was sad, however, that she had to give up her job at The Vixen Den. Her mother had pointed out that with the mages in New

York, they could attack her there and possibly get some of her friends hurt. Mr. G was also disappointed, but told her that she could come back anytime she wanted.

"Enjoying yourself, Astrid?" Adrianna peered at her over the newspaper she was reading.

"Thoroughly," she answered saucily, then covered her mouth. "Sorry. Am I eating too much? I don't mean to seem so crude. This is a really nice jet, and your food is delicious."

Adrianna chuckled. "Not at all. Please, help yourself. It's the least I can do after my overprotective brother roped you into this. But," her eyes darted to the galley. "Steve's not on the menu. And he's actually on *our* team, I'm afraid."

"Ha!" *Oh why were all the hot ones gay?* She gulped her champagne down. "I like you, Adrianna." And she really did. Astrid had only spent one day shadowing the future Lupa of New Jersey, but she found Adrianna to be smart, capable, and had a no-nonsense attitude. "I want to be you when I grow up."

"Thank you. And I like you, too, Astrid." She put her paper down. "I hope you don't find this all boring though, I really am sorry you got into this mess."

"How could you be so calm after what happened?" Astrid couldn't help the shiver that ran down her spine. "The mages tried to kidnap you, and you're here, business as usual."

"It's not the first time that happened," Adrianna said, her voice going quiet.

"What?" She nearly spit out her champagne. "What do you mean?

Adrianna leaned forward. "It's not a big secret or anything, though my parents try to keep the details on the down-low. Obviously, as the children of the most powerful Alphas in the world and the CEO of a multinational corporation, my siblings and I are targets for lots of unsavory people. When Lucas and I were ten, we were abducted as we were leaving school."

"No! Was it the mages?"

She shook her head. "No, just your garden variety kidnappers for ransom. They shot our bodyguard, Shane, and he almost died." Adrianna's face grew pale, but she took a deep calming breath. "They'd kept us for a few hours, and that's when ..."

"When what?" Astrid asked.

Adrianna's gaze dropped to her lap. "That was the first time Lucas shifted. In bloodlust."

"Wait, he was ten years old?" Astrid asked in disbelief. "But our kind don't usually shift until we're thirteen or fourteen."

"I know," she said. "I didn't shift until I was fourteen. But Lucas ... you see, I couldn't stop crying and the kidnappers didn't know what to do. One them smacked me in the face, and Lucas just lost it."

"Shit!" Astrid shot to her feet and sat down in the chair next to Adrianna. "You poor thing!"

"Nick and your mother came in just in time," she said. "Before Lucas could kill those men. He'd hurt them real bad, though." She wiped her palms on her skirt. "I think that's why he hates humans."

"He hates humans?" she echoed.

"Yeah. I mean, he'd never say it, of course. But except for our best friend, Hannah, his only other close friends are Lycans, or hybrids, or other magical people. He never liked any of my human ex-boyfriends. He only tolerates those he has to work with and as far as I know, never even dated anyone who wasn't Lycan."

"Huh." That made sense, kind of. He was only ten years old and his only experience with humans outside the Lycan world had been horrific. "Well I—"

"Good morning, ladies."

Astrid's spine went rigid at the sound of the voice. She looked over her shoulder. "What the hell are you doing here?"

"Yes, I'm having a lovely day, Astrid," Zac said in a droll voice. He strode into the jet and sat down on the seat opposite her. "Hello, Adrianna, are you feeling better?"

"Loads," she said, straightening in her seat. "Thanks for offering to come, Zac. I know Lucas appreciates you taking time away from your busy schedule to escort me."

"Escort you?" Astrid asked.

"Yes," Adrianna said. "Usually Lucas, Uncle Dante, or one of my male cousins attend these events with me, at least for the first night."

"The restaurant industry is still a boy's club unfortunately," Zac continued. "And a lot of these restaurant executives and bad boy chefs just can't take no for an answer, especially from a woman."

Adrianna sighed. "A couple years back, some drunk guy followed me back to my room and nearly broke the door down. So, since then, I've always had an escort, just to send the signal that I'm not there alone."

"That's just awful," Astrid said. "You'd think that in this day and age, you wouldn't have to worry about things like this."

"I've told them lots of times I can take care of myself," she said. "But, since I've refused any kind of regular security detail, this is my compromise with my parents. Lucas had to stay behind, and Zac happened to be free."

"How convenient." Astrid sank back into the chair and crossed her arms over her chest.

"Excuse me," Adrianna stood up. "I need to check on something. I'll be right back. We should be taking off soon." She headed to the rear of the plane.

"What are you doing here, Zac?" The words spilled out of her mouth as soon as she was sure Adrianna was out of earshot.

"I'm here to escort Adrianna and keep those overly amorous chefs away from her." He suddenly lunged toward her, his hands landing on the armrests of her chair to trap her. "Of course, if you're bored, we could always entertain ourselves by joining the mile-high club."

Astrid ignored the shot of heat that went straight to her core. "I don't know. I'd rather have someone who's already a member show me the ropes. Like that hot steward who gets me chocolates and champagne."

His eyes darkened and he leaned close to her, his lips barely brushing her earlobe. "You really are asking for a spanking, aren't you, Astrid?"

She was practically creaming her panties at the thought of being bent over Zac's knee. And from the way his breath hitched, he knew it. *Goddamn him!*

"Zac, please," she whispered.

"Please what, Astrid?" His breath was hot on her skin. "Don't stop?"

"I—"

"Hello! Sorry I'm late!"

Zac pushed himself off the chair and landed back in his own seat. "Who the—Isabelle?"

Astrid looked up. *Motherfucker fuck a duck!* "What are you doing here?"

Isabelle shot daggers at her. "My mother owns this plane, what the hell are *you* doing here?"

"Technically, Muccino International owns this plane," Adrianna said as she walked back into the cabin. "Isabelle, I said you could come along if you arrived on time and you *behaved.*"

"I did come on time. You said we were taking off at noon."

"Which means you come here at least an hour before," Adrianna retorted.

"Well, I'm here, aren't I?" Isabelle's cherry red lips curled up into a sweet smile.

"Why are you here?" Zac said.

"It's been so long since I've been skiing in Vail." She sauntered over to the empty seat beside Zac. "I thought I'd go since Adrianna was taking the jet anyway."

"And what did Grant have to say?" Zac asked.

Isabelle placed a hand on his arm. "Actually, he thought it was a good idea. So did your dad."

"They did?" Astrid asked.

"Yes." She looked at Adrianna. "And I'll be bringing along two guards. And if one of them happened to be around you—"

Adrianna's mismatched eyes blazed. "What? Those sneaky ... can't believe he would do that. He knows how I feel about having someone follow me around."

"Stop being stubborn, Adrianna." Isabelle flipped her hair. "I don't even know why you refuse to have a bodyguard. They're so handy when I need privacy while shopping and for holding my bags."

"The men and women of the Lycan Security Team aren't your personal servants, Isabelle," Adrianna said. "It's wasteful and unnecessary to have two guards on you."

"Whatever. It's too late." She motioned behind them toward the plane's door where two burly men were coming on board, suitcases in hand. "They're here. And we're about to take off, right? You wouldn't want to delay takeoff, would you, Adrianna?"

Adrianna grabbed her seatbelt and yanked it across her lap. "You can bet I'll be talking to Papa when we land."

A few more minutes passed, and soon they were in the

air. Once they reached cruising altitude, Steve came out to serve them lunch.

"Thank you, Steve," Astrid drawled as the handsome steward poured her another glass of champagne. Zac's mouth twisted into a scowl, though when Isabelle began to flirt with him and draw him into a conversation, he turned his attention to the younger woman.

Astrid sat back and crossed her arms over her chest. No, she was not jealous of Isabelle. Not at all, despite the fact that it took all her might to rein in her wolf, who was roaring to get out and rip Isabelle to pieces.

"Excuse me," she murmured as she got out of her chair and headed for the lavatory. She went inside and though she wanted to stay there even after she was finished freshening up, she knew she had to get out eventually. When she pushed the door open, she was surprised when she bumped into something very solid. "I—ugh!" It was Zac of course, and when he didn't move out of her way, she pushed at his chest.

"Where's the fire, Astrid?" he asked, capturing her wrists. "I think Steve's a little busy, but if you're still looking for someone to show you the ropes—"

"Just get out of my way," she bit out, yanking her hands away. When she sidestepped to move away from him, he moved into the lavatory past her, brushing his body against hers. "I—" But before she could complete her sentence, the door slammed in her face. *Asshole.*

She made her way back to the main cabin and slunk down into her seat. Isabelle's nostrils flared and her gaze narrowed. "Nice pants, Astrid. Did you get those at the Big and Tall shop?"

She stared down at her baggy stonewashed jeans, which probably had been Cross or Gunnar's at some point. "Nice bag, Isabelle." She pointed her chin at the bag that lay at the younger woman's feet. It was pink with a fluffy fur lining. "Did you skin a cat from the shelter to make it?"

Isabelle's eyes flashed with anger. "At least I'm not wearing hand me—"

"Isabelle!" Adrianna warned. "Apologize to Astrid, now."

"She insulted my bag!"

"You started it," her sister said. "Do it or you'll be headed home with this plane."

"Fine." She pouted at Astrid. "I'm sorry."

Her tone didn't sound sorry at all, but Astrid was not in the mood, so she murmured an acceptance and put her seatbelt on.

Zac came back shortly after, and as soon as he sat down, Isabelle once again turned on the charm. Astrid grabbed the nearest magazine within her reach and opened it to the first page. She convinced herself that the article on enhancing restaurant efficiency with the latest POS system really was riveting and enjoyable, despite the fact that she had read the same paragraph five times without really understanding it.

"Actually, if you ladies don't mind, I have to make a conference call," Zac said as he stood up. "I'll be in the bedroom. I should be wrapped up right before we land."

"Don't be too long, Zac," Isabelle cooed after him. As soon as he was gone, she grabbed her phone and began to tap the screen with rapid-fire efficiency.

Astrid breathed a sigh of relief, as she really didn't think she could stand hearing Isabelle's voice for the next three hours. The time passed quicker than she thought it would, and she estimated that they must be landing soon. Sure enough, Steve came out of the galley.

"I'm sorry," the steward began. "The captain asked me to inform you that we'll be delayed another thirty minutes."

"Thirty minutes?" Adrianna's delicate brow shot up. "Why?"

"Some dignitary had to leave and has tied up the runway. I do apologize."

Adrianna sighed. "It's not your fault, Steve. I guess we'll just have to wait."

Astrid was not looking forward to spending another minute in the jet, and she briefly wondered if her Lycan body would be able to survive the freezing temperatures outside the plane, if she *poofed* herself on the wing. *Probably not.*

———

The delay in landing wasn't as long as the captain had predicted, which Astrid was grateful for. A car picked them up from the private airstrip, and after battling some traffic, they finally arrived at the Blue Mountain Ski Resort in Vail. It was the perfect day for skiing—bright skies, white powder snow, and the air was fresh and clean. No wonder the resort was busy, plus there was the conference going on. As soon as they entered, however, Zac excused himself, saying he needed to find a private place to conduct a phone call.

Astrid stood in the corner with their bags, while Adrianna went to the front desk, refusing to let the bodyguards check them in. She really admired Adrianna, that despite her upbringing, she remained grounded and humble. In fact, most of the Anderson siblings did. Except—

"Oh my God, Maxie, I'm soooo disappointed," Isabelle said as she came up to where Astrid was waiting. She had her smartphone up to her face, teetering on her stiletto boots as the two bodyguards walked behind her, their arms full of luggage and bags. "So, I heard from Brianna, who heard from Shaylene, who heard from the bellman that His Highness *just* left."

"Prince Karim?" Maxine's high-pitched squeal made the tinny speakers on Isabelle's phone crackle. "But he was supposed to be opening that club you were going to tonight, right?"

"I know, I'm soooo annoyed." Isabelle's delicate nose wrinkled. "He had some business back in his kingdom or something. He's the reason we had to circle around before landing."

"Well, now I don't feel so bad I couldn't come to Vail with you," Maxine said.

"Yeah, now I'm stuck with—" When her mismatched

eyes landed on Astrid, she turned away, but murmured something about "man pants."

"Isabelle," Adrianna barked as she approached them. "Get your goons to take your bags up to our suite."

"*Our* suite?" the younger woman whined. "Papa said I could have my own room."

"Yeah, well change of plans." She handed Astrid a keycard. "Astrid will take the single suite and you'll be bunking in with me."

"B-b-but Papa—"

"I'm sure he'll be relieved to know your two guards will only have to monitor one room," Adrianna pointed out.

"Fine." She grabbed the keycard her sister offered to her. "I'll see you later." She sauntered away, her two Lycan guards following in her wake.

Adrianna shook her head. "It's a fourteen hundred square foot suite! You'd have thought I was asking her to move into a hostel with ten bunk beds."

"I would have been happy sharing the suite with you, Adrianna," Astrid said. "Clearly if she's unhappy—"

Adrianna tsked. "No, no. She has to learn she can't always have her way. *Madre de dio.*" She shook her head. "My parents—or rather, my father—spoil her way too much."

"Maybe she'll grow out of it."

"I hope so." Adrianna took her hand. "Now, about tonight."

"What about tonight?"

"There's a reception for all the attendees."

"Oh, right." That was something she should have known as Adrianna's 'assistant.' "So, did you need me to chill out or maybe stalk the security room."

"No," Adrianna said. "I'll need you in there with me."

Astrid's heart dropped. "Um, I'm not really good in those situations. Plus, I don't have anything to wear."

"Don't worry about that," Adrianna said. "I always bring a few extra clothes."

She didn't want to point out that Adrianna was about five inches shorter than her. "But—"

"*Ay, basta*." Adrianna clucked her tongue. "You want to be able to keep an eye on me, right?"

"I suppose."

"It's settled then." Adrianna straightened her shoulders. "Now, I'll have someone send the dress up to your room. Do you need makeup or anything? You can go ahead and buy some from the gift shop, and just charge it to our account."

"I should be fine. I'll make sure not to embarrass you as your date," she joked.

"Oh, no worries. Zac is my real date for this one. Okay, I'll see you later."

Adrianna hurried off before her words had fully sunk into Astrid's brain. *Oh, mother of all that was holy*. How could she have forgotten that Zac would be there as well? She groaned inwardly. *Maybe I'll develop a pox before evening*. But then again, she wasn't that lucky. She just hoped she wouldn't be embarrassed like she had been five years ago.

CHAPTER ELEVEN

Zac checked his reflection in the mirror one last time. He was glad he always traveled with a tux, just in case. It came in very handy this time around.

He thought it would have been difficult for him to somehow get an invitation to come to Vail, but it turned out easier than he thought. The day after the attack, he had overheard his father, the Alpha, and Lucas discussing Adrianna's arrangements for the conference. Nick was getting ready to be her escort, but Zac stepped in and volunteered instead. "You need to stay here and start making plans for our defense against the mages," he had said. "You were one of the few that fought them, and the Alpha will need your expertise."

Astrid was obviously not happy to see him step on that plane, so he did enjoy watching her squirm in jealousy around Isabelle. Of course, he couldn't stand being around the girl. It really was uncomfortable, the way Isabelle flirted heavily with him. Besides, his inner wolf was annoyed with her and with him, and it would not stand for Astrid being unhappy. He had thought Astrid had been serious about Steve, but when he saw the steward checking *him* out and sending heavy-lidded glances his way, he knew he had nothing to worry about, and his own jealousy had been tampered down.

After a final check, Zac left his room, jiggling the knob just to be sure it was safely locked. As he looked up, he stopped at the sight that greeted him across the hall. He stood there, transfixed at the vision before him.

The last time that he had seen Astrid that afternoon was when they arrived at the hotel. He was pulled into another last-minute conference call and by the time he was done, the ladies had all checked in. Adrianna had messaged him the details of what time he had to be ready to come by her room, but nothing else. He had assumed that only he and Adrianna were going to be at tonight's party.

Astrid looked nothing like she did before; well, except maybe the first time he saw her again a few days ago in that ridiculously sexy robe. Red was obviously a good color on her. The crimson off-the-shoulder dress she wore showed off an expanse of creamy skin and just a hint of cleavage. The fabric clung tight around her torso and rest of her body and would have probably been constricting were it not for the high slit on the side. She turned around to make sure her door was secure, exposing a long, slim leg.

His mouth went dry, thinking of the last time she had those legs wrapped around him. She was like a flame, drawing him in like a moth, and he found himself standing inches from her. When she did turn around to face him, her beautiful whiskey-colored eyes lit up in surprise.

"Zac."

The mere sound of his name on her lips was enough to make him hard as steel, and he was glad he had thought to button his coat. "Astrid." He took one step closer to her, and while he saw her nostrils flare, she didn't cower or look intimidated, which drove him even wilder. "You look beautiful." She only wore a touch of make-up, maybe something to make her lips glossy, but that was about it. Her hair was swept to one side and tumbled in waves down her left shoulder.

He half expected her to brush him off or say something rude, so he was surprised when she said, "T-thank you. You look nice too."

"Zac. Astrid. Good, you're both here."

He whipped his head around and found Adrianna standing next to one of the doors behind him. "Adrianna," he greeted. "I didn't know Astrid would be joining the party as well."

"She's supposed to be my assistant." Adrianna walked toward them, her long, green gown flowing behind her. "Don't you look lovely, Astrid," she greeted. "I'm glad my dress fit you."

"Thanks," Astrid answered. "It's a little, uh, revealing. Maybe I should change or something—"

"Maybe you should." Zac frowned. No wonder that slit was so high, seeing as Adrianna was much shorter than Astrid. He could practically see Astrid's tonsils, which meant all of the men downstairs would too.

Adrianna laughed, her mismatched eyes sparkling. "Don't be silly, we're going to be late." She hooked her arm around Zac's. "In fact, we should get going." As they started down the hallway, Adrianna shook her head. "Oh, come on now, Zac, be a gentleman." She gave a pointed look toward Astrid, who was trailing behind them.

"Of course." He extended his free arm toward Astrid, and though she hesitated for a moment, she took it anyway. From this close, he could stare down at Astrid and get a good view of her cleavage. When her hair brushed his shoulder, he got a whiff of her intoxicating scent and nearly stumbled.

"Everything okay, Zac?" Adrianna asked with an amused smile on her face.

"Why, yes, Adrianna," he answered back. "Why don't we head downstairs." Inwardly, he groaned. This would be a long night.

They went down to the hotel ballroom where the reception was taking place. Once they were signed in, they all walked in together. He let Adrianna lead him around as she networked and hobnobbed, but Astrid had somehow broken away from them. By the time he realized this, it was too late.

He and Adrianna were across the room and Astrid was standing by the bar, sipping on a drink. The predators were already circling, and he noticed a few of the men checking out Astrid, waiting to pounce. He gritted his teeth when he saw a distinguished older man he recognized as a judge from some British cooking reality show strike up a conversation with her.

When he volunteered to help keep Adrianna safe from the overly amorous men at the conference, he didn't think he'd have to worry about who would protect Astrid.

"Zac, did you hear me?"

He frowned and then turned back to Adrianna. "Could you repeat what you said?"

Adrianna smiled slyly at him. "Oh, it was nothing important."

He grimaced. "Sorry."

"You seemed distracted this evening. Got something on your mind?"

Did Adrianna know about him and Astrid? She looked amused, and there was no doubt about his friend's intelligence. Of course, he didn't know himself what was happening between him and Astrid. "No, I'm fine." But he couldn't help himself as he looked over to Astrid again. The reality show star was now leaning over her, his eyes fixed on her chest. His inner wolf, normally silent at public gatherings like this, made its displeasure known with a snarl.

Adrianna followed his gaze. "You should go over there and rescue her."

"Huh? I mean—" he cleared his throat, "I'm here to keep you safe."

She rolled her eyes. "Why do the men in my life think I can't take care of myself? Most of the people here know me already. Now," she shooed him away. "Go. Ask her to dance."

He didn't have to be told twice. And if Adrianna suspected something—so what? He was an adult and so was Astrid. They could make their own decisions. And right now, it looked like Astrid was making a bad one as she moved closer to the man whose eyes were so far down between her breasts, they might as well have detached from their sockets. His wolf pushed him on, urging him to get that other male away from her.

"—how about we go up to my suite?" Mr. Reality Show star whispered. "I can have champagne brought up to my room."

Astrid smiled up sweetly at him as she sidled closer. "Now, Mr. Brown, as I said—" she brushed her hand up the lapel of his tux. "I. Am. Not. Interested!"

Mr. Brown's eyes crossed as she put a well-placed knee between his legs. He let out a muffled cry and doubled over. Zac signaled to one of the Lycan bodyguards who had been watching over Adrianna—a man he recognized as Keith Johnson— as he quickly made his way to Astrid's side.

"Let's go and dance," he whispered in her ear. She sounded like she wanted to protest, but let out a small squeak when he slid a hand around her waist and pulled her away. Meanwhile, the stern-faced Johnson wrapped a meaty hand around Mr. Brown's mouth before pulling him out of the room.

Zac brought them to the middle of the dance floor, twisting her around so she faced him. "That wasn't very nice," she said. "Having Johnson drag that poor man away like a sack of potatoes."

"What you did wasn't nice either," he pointed out. He brushed a lock of hair away from her face.

"The things he said ..." she frowned.

"What did he say?" he asked, gripping her waist tighter.

She huffed. "Let's just say, I understand why Adrianna needs an escort to these things. Hey—what are you doing?"

He held up her right hand, which he had taken in his. "Dancing."

"Dancing?" She looked confused. "With whom?"

He swayed her back and forth. "With you, of course."

"But I can't dance. I—"

Before she could say anything else, he released her waist, twirled her around, then pulled her back. "See? You can dance."

She smirked at him. "I think you're the one dancing. I'm merely swaying along with you."

"And you do it so well." He pressed her body just a bit closer, wondering if she would try to wiggle away or worse —give him the same treatment as the unlucky Mr. Brown.

What he didn't expect was for her to relax against him. She seemed almost contented. "Did you learn to dance?"

She guffawed. "My mom tried to send me to dance lessons. You could probably guess how that turned out. Where did you learn to dance, anyway?"

"My great-grandfather insisted on it. He said it was one of those 'Old World social graces' that everyone had to learn if he was going to be a respectable man." The music changed to a song with a slower beat. So, he changed their rhythm, and moved his hand to her lower back, just above the curve of her ass. He pulled her forward so she brushed up right against him.

"This doesn't feel very respectable." She looked down between them, where their bodies touched. "Haven't you heard of 'leaving room for Jesus'?"

"I never said I was respectable," he whispered in her ear. As they danced, he looked around them and saw a door that probably led to the balcony outside. *Perfect.* No one would be out there because of the freezing temperatures. He maneuvered her backward, away from the dance floor and the other people.

"Zac?" She looked up at him with curious eyes. "Where are we—" She took in a deep breath when the balcony doors opened behind them, the cold wind rushing in. He wrapped an arm around her as he walked her back, then closed the doors behind him. "It's freezing out here!" she exclaimed.

"Here." He took off his coat and wrapped it around her shoulders. It was a useless gesture as Astrid's body would warm up on its own, but he couldn't help it. She was beautiful in her dress, but even more so with his tuxedo jacket covering her up. It would also mean she'd be covered in his scent, which pleased his inner wolf to no end.

"Thanks," she said, pulling the jacket closer around her. "Care to tell me what we're doing out here?"

"It was getting stuffy in there," he said. "And I didn't get a chance to warm you up that night on the balcony."

"Because you thought I was making out with someone else," she pointed out.

"Well—"

"My *brother*," she added.

"He did just show up out of nowhere. But now that it's just us—"

"Zac." She placed her hands on his chest. "Please. Don't."

"Don't what?"

"Don't do this." She swallowed visibly. "You know this can't work between us."

"Why do you keep saying that?"

"Because it's true!" She pushed him away. "I don't know what you want from me. We have nothing in common, and we're worlds apart. I've done nothing to make you want me, and you're not being fair."

Her words made him freeze. Aside from the consuming attraction between them, what else was there between them? What would happen if they did give in? "Do you want a relationship? Is that it?"

"What?" She seemed horrified at the thought, which

wounded his pride even more. "No, I … I'm … You've ignored me for years, and now I'm supposed to believe that you're attracted to me all of a sudden?"

He grabbed the lapels of the jacket and brought her closer to him. "Wait, what do you mean 'ignored you'? I've barely seen you."

"That's it," she sighed. "You haven't seen me at all."

She turned away, but he pulled her back to face him. "What are you saying, Astrid?"

"I want to go back to my room, Zac," she said.

"Not until you tell me what this is about."

"What are you going to do? Keep me hostage here?" she challenged.

It sounded real tempting right now, though he wished they were somewhere warmer and more private. "Astrid, talk to me."

"There's nothing to talk about, Zac." She wrenched free of him, then took off his jacket and laid it on the railing. "I'm tired. I'm going to head back to my room. And you should go back to Adrianna."

He stood there, frozen to the spot, and not just because of the temperatures. What in God's name had Astrid been talking about? What did she mean he didn't see her at all?

When he finally shook himself out of his reverie, he gathered enough sense to head back inside. Astrid was nowhere to be seen, as she probably did head upstairs. The need to go there and bang on her door was great; his wolf was clawing at him, furious that he let her go. However, if there was anything he'd learned in the past few days, it was that the more he pushed Astrid, the more she would fight him. Somehow, he had to let her come to him. *But how?*

———

It was another sleepless night, but then again what was new? Ever since that night Zac saw Astrid, he couldn't get a good night's sleep. He lay in bed, wondering what it was he did to her. It was obvious it was *something,* but what? He was determined to find out.

He was supposed to go back home this morning, but if he wanted answers, he had to stay. So, he called the pilot and told him to cancel their flight back home, telling him that it didn't seem practical to have the jet fly him back to New York today, only to then come back and get Adrianna the next day.

After sending emails and a long call to his assistants back in London, he got dressed and finally left his room. Just his damned luck, Isabelle was also on her way out.

"Zac!" she called, running down the hall toward him, dressed in her designer ski suit. "Oh, Zac, good thing I caught you!"

"What is it, Isabelle?" He couldn't even bring himself to be nice to her this morning.

"I thought you were supposed to leave this morning?"

"It seemed like a waste of fuel for the to jet go back and forth in twenty-four hours," he explained. "So I decided to stay until tomorrow."

"Oh great!" She clapped her hands together. "That

means we can go skiing!"

He shook his head. "I'm too busy for skiing, Isabelle. Can't you go on your own?"

"Please, Zac?" She batted her eyelashes at him. "I don't want to go alone. Neither of my bodyguards know how to ski. What if something happened to me? Those mages are out to get us, right?"

He gritted his teeth. Spending the day on the slopes with Isabelle was the last thing he wanted to do, but he had no doubt that she would insist on going out anyway without her bodyguards. Besides, Adrianna and Astrid would be busy at the conference today and he didn't have a ticket to attend. "Fine," he said. Maybe some exercise would do him good and release some of the tension he'd been feeling. "I'll meet you at the gear rental place in half an hour, after I call the office to let them know I'll be out."

"Yay!" she squealed, then jumped up to kiss him on the cheek. "Thanks, Zac, you won't regret this!" She ran down the hall, humming happily to herself as she went into the elevator.

As promised, Zac showed up at the ski rental hut half an hour later. Isabelle was already there waiting for him. "I knew you'd come," she said smugly. "Oh, I can't wait to get out onto the slopes."

He gave his shoe size to the clerk behind the counter. "We're not spending the whole day skiing, Isabelle," he said. "I have to get back after lunch."

"Boo." Isabelle pouted. "You're no fun."

"You should listen to your friend," the clerk said as he handed Zac a pair of boots. "They're saying there might be a freak storm coming in later today."

"See, Isabelle?" Zac said. "We'll take a couple runs and then head back."

"Ugh, who cares? I've been skiing double black diamonds since I was thirteen." She grabbed her gear. "C'mon, Zac, let's go."

He followed her out to the slopes and lined up for the ski lifts. While he let her chatter on incessantly as they made their way to the top of the slope, he had to admit, it was beautiful out here. It reminded him of one vacation they had over the winter break when he was fourteen. They had gone to Switzerland, all of them, even his great-grandfather. The hurt lessened after all these years of him being gone, but it was still there.

"Zac!" Isabelle called as she hopped off the lift and scooted away.

Lost in his own thoughts, he nearly missed the jump. "I'm right behind you."

"You're such a head case today," she said, walking over to the first slope. "Well, forget about whatever's bothering you. Let's go!" Isabelle pulled her goggles over her face, planted her poles onto the snow and then pushed herself off. Zac huffed and then followed the younger woman down the slope.

The resort's intermediate course was challenging, even

for an experienced skier like himself. Isabelle didn't seem to have any trouble navigating the steep slopes, zooming down with ease. When they reached the bottom, Isabelle insisted they head up again right away to the more difficult runs. He had to admit, he was having fun, and it had been years since he'd done anything so exhilarating. It was almost like having the freedom to shift and run in his wolf form as he pleased. When was the last time he did that anyway? Too long.

Though he was enjoying himself, Zac knew that they couldn't stay too long. The dark clouds were already coming closer, and flurries had built up around them as they did their last descent. Zac told Isabelle it was time to head back.

"But we've only done a couple of runs!" she whined.

"Isabelle, I told you I can't stay too long. Besides," he pointed to the gray skies in the distance. "I think that guy at the rental place was right. There might be a snowstorm coming."

"Oh, boo!" She made a face. "I'm going one last time on the double black diamond course. You can join me or not, but if something happens, then you'll have to explain to my father, your *Alpha*, why I was alone." She marched off in the direction of the ski lifts.

Zac considered letting the brat just go off on her own, but he knew if anything did happen to her, he would no doubt feel guilty. With a deep sigh, he followed behind her.

"I knew you'd cave in," Isabelle said as he sat down on

the lift chair. "All this snow ... this last one is going to be great, I know it."

"One last run and then we're headed inside, okay?"

"You're so grumpy and serious, Zac." She rubbed his arm. "C'mon, when was the last time you had fun?"

"I have plenty of fun." The chair lurched forward and he grabbed the side to prevent himself from falling over. As they ascended up the mountain, he couldn't help but wonder about Astrid. The physical exertion helped keep his mind off her, but when it was quiet like this, his thoughts drifted to her.

"Ready?" Isabelle said as they neared the top of the most advanced slope in the resort. There was no one else there, and the snow was now whipping around them.

"I think we should take the lifts back, Isabelle." There was a feeling in his gut, and it wasn't good.

"Don't be a sissy!" she taunted. "C'mon!" With a loud whoop, she pushed herself off and disappeared down the mountain.

Zac let out an exasperated sound and put his goggles on. He followed her down the mountain, zooming down the powdery slopes at top speed. The wind was really coming in fast now, blowing snowflakes around him. Good thing Isabelle was easy to spot in her hot pink ski suit, so he was able to follow, but she was so fast that eventually, he could no longer see the bright blur in front of him.

They had done this run a couple of times now, so he knew the course well enough. However, he knew there were a few dangerous curves, even for seasoned skiers, plus the weather seemed to get worse and worse by the second. The bad feeling in Zac's gut grew and he bent down lower, trying to pick up speed. When he heard the loud *whump* sound behind him, he knew he was in deep trouble. That sound meant only one thing: snow dislodging from the side of the mountain. An avalanche.

CHAPTER TWELVE

"I hope you weren't too bored." Adrianna closed her laptop and put it away in her bag.

"What? Nah, I'm fine," Astrid replied. "Thanks for letting me hang out. And I never knew the restaurant industry was so ... uh ..."

"Dry?" Adrianna finished with a smile. "Tedious? Dull?"

She laughed. "Okay fine, I did find myself drifting off a couple of times." When she woke up that morning, she really didn't know what she was supposed to do today. There was nothing else to do at the resort but ski, which she hadn't done since she was a kid.

So, instead of staying in her room bored out of her mind, she asked Adrianna if she could tag along with her during the conference. Honestly, she wasn't sure what to expect, but it was just one long and boring talk after another.

Still, she probably would have gone stir crazy inside her room all day, especially after last night. *I can't believe I almost told him about that incident.* It seemed like a long time ago, but the memory of it still made her cringe. Good thing it was only Deedee who witnessed her embarrassment.

"So, did you want to have dinner later?" Adrianna asked as they left the meeting room. "I did set up a few one-on-one meetings before five, but we could meet at the restaurant, say around six?"

"Sure." Not that she had plans. And since Zac had left that morning, she should be sticking to Adrianna, at least until they were back in New York. "How about—"

"Miss Anderson!"

They both turned around at the sound of the voice. "Keith?" Adrianna said as the Lycan guard approached them.

Keith Johnson had a scowl on his face, which only deepened when he spoke. "There's been an accident on the slopes. Please come with me."

"Is it Isabelle?" The panic in Adrianna's voice was evident. "Oh God, is it the mages?"

He shook his head. "No, Miss Anderson. She's all right. It's Mr. Vrost."

"Zac?" Astrid couldn't stop herself. "What happened? Tell us right now!"

"Mr. Vrost and Miss Anderson were out on the slopes, apparently," he began. "And there was an avalanche. Miss

Anderson made it down, but no one's heard from Mr. Vrost since."

Her heart stopped for a second as she listened to Keith relay the story, and then began to pound against her chest. *Oh God.*

"But Zac was supposed to go home this morning," Adrianna said. "I don't understand."

"He cancelled his flight," Keith answered. "Anyway, we should go to the resort manager's office. Miss Anderson is there."

Astrid's entire body felt numb. All she could think about was Zac, buried under a ton of snow. His Lycan body would allow him to survive for a few hours in the cold, but they weren't invincible. Without shelter, he could still freeze to death if the temperatures went down enough.

"Astrid? Astrid?" Adrianna's face was grave with concern. "Are you all right?"

"Yes, I'm ... Zac, he ..." She swallowed the lump growing in her throat. Her head was spinning, but she needed to stay calm. "Let's go find out more."

Keith led them to the manager's office, where Isabelle was already sitting down in one of the chairs, sobbing uncontrollably. "Adrianna!" She jumped up and ran to her sister. Adrianna enveloped her in a hug, whispering soothing words in her ear.

"Now," Adrianna began as she led Isabelle back to her chair. "Explain what happened."

As Isabelle told the story of what happened that morning

between tears and sobs, Astrid listened intently. According to the younger woman, they had been out on one last run on the double black diamond course when the storm started picking up, then she heard the rumblings of the avalanche. She thought Zac was just behind her and she barely escaped the deluge of snow that had covered nearly half of the course.

"I swear, he wasn't far behind," Isabelle cried. "I just thought ..."

Astrid's inner wolf howled in anger and fear. *Stupid, selfish Isabelle!* But there was no time for blaming now. With each minute that Zac was out there, his chances of surviving were getting smaller and smaller.

"We have all the ski patrol and rescue workers out there looking for him and other survivors," the resort manager said. "We're doing our best."

Astrid looked out the window. It had grown darker in the last couple of minutes and the snow was not letting up. Their best wasn't good enough. She pulled Adrianna aside. "Call your dad. And my dad too."

"I'm already on it." Adrianna held up her phone.

"Good." She turned and headed out the door.

"Wait, Astrid, where are you going?"

"I'm going to try and find him."

"What?" Adrianna grabbed her arm. "Are you crazy? You could get lost too!"

"I can't just let him .... I mean, if he ..." She bit her lip, trying to swallow down the burning tears in her throat. *Think!* She took a deep breath. "Keith," she called to the guard. "You have your tracker with you?"

"Yes." He pulled back his suit sleeve, revealing a thin black band. All members of the Lycan Security Team wore special bracelets that expanded as they shifted and contained a GPS tracking device.

"Good. Give it to me." The guard hesitated, but when Adrianna nodded, handed it over to Astrid. "Now, I'll go out and search for Zac in my wolf form. You can keep track of me via the bracelet and then send my dad or Cross after me."

"Why don't we have Keith go out and look for him?"

"I'll be fine," she said. "Look, the mages aren't after me or Zac. We'll be fine, but if they do know you're here and unprotected, they might seize the opportunity. You need Keith here."

The other woman looked defeated. "I don't like this."

"You don't have to like it," Astrid said. "But you can't stop me."

"Astrid," Adrianna began. "I know that you feel—"

"I should go," she interrupted. "Let's not waste any more time. Trust me, I can take care of myself. I can always *poof* myself away from danger." She didn't bother waiting for Adrianna to stop her, but instead, walked away with a determined stride.

Although her wolf wanted her to rush out now, she knew that she had to have some sort of plan in place. *Okay, first things first.* She walked around the resort until she found people wearing ski patrol and rescue team gear, heading toward the "employees only" area of the resort.

Aside from just teaching her how to fight, her former

Lone Wolf uncles also taught her and her cousins other useful skills from their less-than-savory pasts. Her mother and three uncles had been raised by a former master thief who trained them in various skills, after all. Her Uncle Killian, for example, could break into any bank, safe, or secure location. He had told her that the best way of getting into any place you weren't supposed to be in was to look like you belonged.

She found another group of rescue workers hanging around the lobby and made a beeline for them. As she passed by, she casually bumped into one of the guys playing on his phone. "Oh, excuse me! I'm so clumsy."

The young man caught her arm and helped steady her. "No worries, ma'am," he said with a bright smile. "Be careful."

"Oh, I will!" She waved at them before turning away, his badge in her fingers. She clipped the badge on her lapel and headed toward the "employees only" area. The rescue workers were already gathered in the middle of the room as an older man stood on a dais in front of a map. Astrid saw a reflective vest lying on one of the chairs and she snatched it up and put it on as she made her way to the front.

"... here," the older man pointed to a spot in the map, "is where we think our guy may have been caught in the avalanche. It's halfway down the double black diamond course. According to our witness...."

Astrid listened for a few minutes, squinting her eyes at the map to commit it to memory. Looks like her study sessions with Uncle Quinn were paying off. As the man began to rattle of more specific instructions, she backed out of the room and made her way outside, to the large rear patio that had a view of the slopes. During the day, this patio was filled with skiers for the *apres-ski* activities, but now it was completely empty.

She looked up the mountain, thinking of the daunting task ahead of her. It had grown much darker since she last checked, but her Lycan vision would help her see in the dim light. The snowstorm was slowing down too, and now only soft flakes fell down from the sky. Hopefully, she wasn't too late.

"Don't think like that," she hissed to herself. "Just find him."

She trudged out into the snow, into the line of trees just off the main outrun. When she was behind the trees, she quickly stripped her clothing off, hanging them from a low branch. She shifted into her wolf form almost too quickly, her animal eager to take over and start looking for Zac. It had barely landed on all fours when it took off, up the mountain.

This was stupid, she thought as her she-wolf ascended up the steep slope. Oh God, what had she been thinking? How would she even know where to find him?

Her wolf let out a yelp and growl, as if to say, "Shut up! I know what I'm doing!" She shrugged and allowed it to take over their body, keeping herself small and quiet inside the wolf's body.

While she already possessed the enhanced senses of her animal even in human form, it was even stronger in animal form. She could hear and smell everything. She also didn't feel tired, despite the energy it took to ascend the mountain. Her she-wolf seemed doggedly determined and single-minded in its mission.

Eventually, they reached the spot where the rescuers had said that Zac could have been caught in the avalanche. The full moon was bright above them and the snow had completely stopped. Where would they start looking?

The she-wolf snapped its jaws, as if telling her to be silent. It perked up its ears, straining to hear something—anything. Astrid closed her eyes, focusing on Zac. *Oh, Zac.* She wished things didn't end the way they had last night. Wished she'd let him kiss her one last time—

The wolf's yelp snapped her out of her thoughts as it dashed up over the mound of snow. She wasn't sure what set off her wolf, but when she concentrated, she heard it—the sound of breathing somewhere underneath the snow. Her animal circled until it settled on a spot, then began to dig. Giant paws clawed at the ground, pushing piles and piles of ice away. The breathing began to get louder, then there was a cough and—

Zac!

A hand popped up and the wolf's mouth opened to grab a sleeve. It pulled with all its might, dragging Zac's body out from under the ice. The wolf whined as it licked his cold face. His skin was freezing and his breathing was labored, but other than that, he was alive. *Thank God!*

The temperatures were still dropping, however, and

his clothes were probably soaked through. She had to get Zac somewhere safe and dry.

In her Lycan form, she was larger than the average gray wolf, but Zac was tall and heavy. But she had to try, so she made her wolf dig under his body and prop him up on her back. With the added weight, she didn't trust her strength enough to make the descent down the slope without slipping and having them roll all the way down. They would be better off taking the rocky path through the trees slowly, stopping to rest if necessary and maybe even finding shelter in a low branch until rescue came.

As they made their way to the dense thicket of trees, she heard a sound from high above them. *Oh, no.* It was that distinct sound of packed snow breaking apart. There would be another avalanche. There was no luxury of time. They had to leave now.

Think, Astrid.

Unless Zac woke up, she would have to drag him down, hopefully before the avalanche caught up to them. What to do? If only she had her father's powers.

No, there's always a solution. That's what her uncles and mother taught her. *Find a way.*

She pictured the map back at the resort in her mind. It showed the main paths of all the courses, which led to the outrun. Near the red X where they had marked Zac's possible location was something ... what was it? Searching through her brain, she didn't know what she was looking for, but knew it was important. Something handwritten in faded ink.

Old ranger's cabin.

If her bearings were correct, there was a cabin not far from where they were right now, due east. *Well, it's now or never. Let's go!*

The she-wolf mustered all its strength to carry Zac on its back and slogged through the snow. *Faster, faster!* There was another loud *whump* sound from behind them and then the ground shook. The wolf whined, but kept on and soon she saw the building in the distance.

Yes!

They pushed on, the wolf moving as fast as it could, and Astrid cheering it on. They were a few steps away from the door when she heard the snow descending on the mountain. *It's okay*, she told her wolf, *I can take it from here. You rest.*

She'd never shifted back to human form so fast in her life. Using the last bit of her strength, she grabbed Zac and hauled him up, dragging him through the door of the cabin and dropped him on the floor with a loud thud. As soon as it shut behind them, the walls shook as mounds of snow fell on top of the cabin. They were trapped, but at least they were safe. She let out a sigh.

The interior of the cabin was sparse. It had a single room, a fireplace in the side, a stove, plus a table and chair pushed up against one wall.

Ack! She looked down and realized she was naked. There was a closet in the corner and she dashed across the room, yanking it open. There was a flannel shirt hanging inside and she quickly grabbed it and put it on, not minding the musty smell. There was also one sleeping bag inside and she picked it up, unrolling it as she dashed back to Zac.

Kneeling down, she unzipped his jacket and pulled it off him. He was breathing more evenly now. *Good.* Lycan healing would stop him from getting hypothermia, but just in case, she took off his wet shoes, socks, and shirt. She supposed she should take his pants off too, but she settled for unbuttoning the fly.

God, she was exhausted. Using the last bit of her strength, she curled up against Zac's chest and threw the sleeping bag over them like a blanket, then closed her eyes.

———

When Astrid regained consciousness, a feeling of disorientation swept over her. For one thing, though her vision was blurred, it was bright. She thought she had dreamt the whole thing. Where was she?

As her sight returned to normal, she saw a roaring fire in front of her. It felt warm too, and so nice after trudging out in the snow. Her body had been nearly numb from being out in the freezing temperatures, and now she could feel everything. Everything, including the hard body pressed up behind her.

"Holy—" She scrambled to her knees. "I—Zac?"

Zac looked up at her lazily, his head propped up on one elbow. A blanket covered him from the waist down, but that was about it. His bare chest and torso were on display, and she couldn't help but stare, her eyes devouring the planes of his broad shoulders, muscled chest, all the way down to the well-defined six-pack abs covered with a sprinkling of dark blond hair that disappeared under the blanket.

"Like what you see?" He grinned up at her.

"I—" God, her cheeks were like a five-alarm fire. "Zac, do you remember what happened?"

"Most of it," he said. "I remember the avalanche and then—you found me and dragged me back here, right? Your wolf did."

She nodded.

"Thank you. I woke up and we were by the door." He gestured to the blanket that had been covering them, as well as the sleeping bag which he must have laid down by the fire. "I managed to find an extra blanket and some firewood too, though that's about the last of it."

The fire was ablaze, but if that was the last of it, then it wouldn't be very long until they would be plunged into the darkness and cold again. She looked out the windows and saw snow covering most of the panes.

"I can't open the door without risking the snow coming in. We're trapped in here for now."

"Shit."

"Do they know we're lost?" he asked.

"Yes, and there are rescue teams looking for us."

"What about your father? Or Cross? Couldn't they just ... show up here and get us out?"

"That's not how their powers work," she said. "It's

similar to mine; they need to have been someplace before or see a clear picture of where they're headed. Wait ... the tracker!" She held up her hand, but found her wrist empty. "Oh, no. Keith gave me his tracker, but I must have lost it in the snow."

"Well, it can't be that far," he said. "Plus, there's rescue teams out looking for us. They might not be able to access the slopes now because of the storm and avalanches, but surely they'll find us by morning."

"Once they locate the tracker, it's only a matter of time." She breathed a sigh of relief. The situation wasn't dire, but they'd have to sit tight until rescue came.

He sat up, his ice blue eyes fixed on her. She suddenly felt self-conscious and tugged the hem of the shirt she was wearing down. It was a futile effort as it came down to the tops of her thighs.

"What were you doing out there, Astrid?" he asked in a quiet voice.

"I was ... looking for you," she confessed. "I was concerned."

A blond brow shot up. "You were concerned?"

"I thought you'd gone back to New York," she explained. "And, well, maybe I thought that you'd stayed ... because of me."

In an instant, he was right beside her, taking her hands into his. "I did." She nearly jumped away from him, but his grip was too strong. "I couldn't go. Not knowing what it is I'd done to you to make you hate me." He pressed his warm lips to the back of her hand.

Her breath caught in her throat at the sensation. "I don't hate you, Zac," she said. "It's ... it's a silly thing. And I was a silly girl. It was also a million years ago."

"If it was all silly and so long ago, why don't you tell me then? When did I ignore you? Because I know if I did see you, there's no way I could have taken my eyes off of you."

She sighed, mesmerized by the light blue orbs of his eyes and the way his lips grazed at the skin of her palms. "You've always ignored me, Zac. At all the functions our families attended. The last one was five years ago at Hannah's wedding. You never made it to her engagement party, but I knew you'd be at the wedding. And ... you had a date."

"I remember bringing someone. And so?"

She slapped her hands over her mouth. "And ... nothing."

He caught her hand again. "Oh no, I'm not letting you get away. Not until you tell me what's wrong. Besides, it's not like you can get away from me now."

She struggled, but he wouldn't let her go. Her shoulders sagged and she let out a deep sigh. "Like I said, this was way back, okay? So, I knew you were going to be at Hannah and Anthony's wedding. It was the biggest affair of the year, after all. Deedee ... she assured me that you weren't with anyone in London and that you wouldn't have a date or anything." She bit her lip. "So, I ... I went and found this dress. It wasn't expensive or anything. Just a nice vintage dress I found at a thrift store. It was all I could afford and ... I went to the wedding and at the reception, I saw you come in ... with your date. Mayor Adkins' daughter."

"Sa ... Sam ... Samantha?" His brows knitted together. "My mother fixed it up. She didn't have a date either. You know Anthony's grandfather was a presidential candidate, right? It was all political, of course, and my parents asked me to take her to the wedding as a good gesture towards the mayor of New York City."

"I *know*." Her gaze shifted to her lap. "I ... I was going to ask you to dance with me."

The look on his face was inscrutable. "Why didn't you?"

Oh God, this was the embarrassing part. "She ... Samantha ... I overheard her in the bathroom. She was talking about how her dress cost hundreds of dollars and how she thought you were so handsome. Everyone around her thought you two made a beautiful couple. And how Cady and Nick would be ecstatic if you ended up with her."

"I ... I didn't know. I didn't even see you there. I mean, I hadn't seen you in years until a few days ago. Astrid. Please, sweetheart, look at me." She lifted her head up. "All I remember of you was this toddler running around Deedee's house at her eighth birthday party. And maybe ... you were maybe twelve or thirteen at one of Fenrir's Christmas parties at the Waldorf Astoria."

"You didn't attend a lot of those parties," she said. "You always went off somewhere on Christmas Eve with your family, except that one time when there was a terrible snowstorm, and you guys couldn't leave. You were seventeen years old, and while the other teens were so sullen and had that 'I'd rather be somewhere else' look, you actually looked happy to be there." She smiled bitterly. "I always thought you looked handsome in a tux, Zac."

"Astrid, even if I did notice you, you would have been way too young for me."

"I wasn't at twenty-one, at the wedding," she pointed out. "In any case, it was then I realized the truth, Zac. We're just too different. You should be with someone like Samantha Adkins—beautiful, smart, and rich and someone who you could be proud of. Not someone like me who—"

"Stop," he growled. "No more." He grabbed her wrists pulled her back to him. "I may have ignored you then, but I won't ignore you now." His hand cupped the back of her neck, his fingers reaching up to dig into her hair. "Astrid, I want you. And I never want you to doubt that." He leaned down to kiss her fiercely, as if he was pouring every bit of passion and emotion into their kiss. She couldn't even bring herself to struggle, and instead, melted into him. Pressed up to him like this, it felt like they were in the blazing Sahara, not the freezing mountains of Colorado.

She moaned into his mouth and reached up to grab his shoulders, clinging to him as she let him plunder her mouth. Her body was yielding to him; she wanted this so bad. And she was so Goddamn tired of ignoring her own needs and wants. When Zac abruptly broke off the kiss, she was left confused.

"Zac?" Her body was still singing with desire. "What's wrong?"

"Absolutely nothing, sweetheart." He sighed and kissed her forehead, then wrapped his arms around her. "I'm sorry for ignoring you that night."

"I was a silly girl," she admitted.

"You. Were. Not." He punctuated each one with a kiss to her lips. "Astrid, I can't explain what's happening here, but please, tell me you feel this too."

She shivered, but nodded. "I don't know what's happening either. But I can't seem to say no to you."

He looked around them. "I know this isn't exactly the most ideal place."

"I've been waiting for years for you to notice me, Zac," she replied in a breathless voice. "Don't make me wait anymore."

"Astrid, we should ... maybe think first. There's a lot going on and I'm afraid—"

She couldn't believe what she was hearing. "Zac, can we just not think, just for tonight? About what's happening out there. We don't know what's ahead, especially with the mages. Just for now ... for tonight, let's not worry about it." She let go of his hand and reached down to grab the hem of the loose shirt, whipping it off in one motion.

He let out a growl, pouncing on top of her and pushing her down on the floor. His hands seemed to be everywhere —on her breasts, her hips, caressing the inside of her thighs. His mouth was rough, devouring hers with such an intensity that she thought she would faint.

When he sat up, he pulled her up with him, barely breaking their kiss. She felt both his hands move lower cupping her ass and lifting her up, wrapping her legs around his waist. His cock was already hard and was pressing up against her lower stomach.

He didn't take her far, didn't even get off his knees. Instead, he crawled them back toward the spread out sleeping bag, laying her down reverently as if it were a pillow-top mattress. When she was on her back, he positioned himself over her, his mouth demanding and claiming.

Her body was on fire, and she couldn't get enough. She moved her hips up, trying to get as much contact with him as possible. A hand came down over her belly, pressing her down, as if to tell her to be patient. His mouth moved lower, down to her jaw, raining kisses all the way to her neck and shoulder blades. She let out a gasp as he licked a path down her breasts, all the way to the pointed tip of her nipple. His hot mouth covered one bud, his tongue teasing it until she was moaning his name. The hand holding down her torso, meanwhile, slid lower. His fingers teased her pussy lips, which were already slick with her own desire. She called his name as he pushed one finger inside her, her hips moving uncontrollably in a rhythmic movement.

He pulled her nipple deeper into his mouth and his hand thrust up against her, meeting the demands of her hips. When his thumb found her clit, she thought she had died and gone to heaven, and the orgasm that washed over her was too much.

"Zac!" she cried out, closing her eyes as her hands turned into fists and pounded down on the floor. As she came down from her orgasm, she let out a sound of disappointment when he pulled his hand away. She reached for him, but only got empty air. When she opened her eyes, she found his head between her thighs, his light blue eyes blazing with desire.

She bit the back of her hand as his mouth caressed her sex. Hot damn, his lips ... that *tongue*. "Uuungh!" Her fingers dug into his hair, tugging at the strands, her hips pushing up at him. He licked at her, relentless and almost punishing, refusing to stop until her body squirmed under his expert ministrations.

"Oh ... sh—" She let out a sharp cry when a powerful orgasm ripped through her. He seemed to revel in her screams of delight, pushing his tongue into her as her body shook with pleasure. "Zac," she moaned. "Please."

He shifted his body, wasting no time or energy in getting between her legs. She was caught in a haze of desire, not caring about the consequences of what tomorrow would bring. When she looked up at him, he was staring right back. The way he looked at her made her heart slam straight into her rib cage.

"Astrid." His voice was rough, and for a moment, she feared he would change his mind. Reaching up, she pulled him down for a kiss, willing him to forget the outside world and just focus on them. She spread her legs to let him come closer, and when she felt the blunt tip of his cock against her entrance, she sighed against his mouth.

Slowly, he filled her. Astrid nearly wept at the care he took, but at the same time it was driving her mad. She relaxed, allowing herself to adjust to his girth. *God, I'm not gonna walk right for* three *weeks.* When he settled inside her, he let out a breath he'd been holding.

She raked her nails down his back lightly, and he let out a growl, his hips slowly drawing out of her. This time, she was the one who held her breath and she nearly gasped when he pushed back inside her.

"Zac! Oh God!" She felt so full, yet still hungry for more. The sensation of being filled like this made her want him so much more. He moved in that sweet rhythm she craved so much. Arching her hips up, she changed the angle of his thrusts.

"You're so perfect, Astrid," he whispered into her ear. "So damn perfect." His cock thrust inside her, in and out, the bones of his hips pressing up just right to grind against her pelvis.

He was really moving hard and fast into her, and she clasped at him, wrapping her legs around his waist as her fingers dug into his shoulders. They were both moaning and gasping, their bodies working hard. The orgasm almost surprised her when it did come—hard and fast, and so deep, she could feel it in her bones. She thought he would be done; hell, after three orgasms she was ready to just collapse. But no, he wanted more.

He pulled her up with him as he sat, adjusting her legs

so she straddled him. His hands wrapped under her arms and hooked over her shoulders so he could pull her down as his cock pounded up into her tight passage. He wouldn't stop, pushing for more. "One more, sweetheart," he groaned. "One more and then I can—"

"Zac!" She moved her hips like a piston, enjoying the feel of his cock sliding in and out of her as the fourth orgasm of the night hit her. He grabbed a fistful of her hair, pulling her head down so she could look at him. His eyes darkened, fixed on her as she came. He let out an animalistic growl and continued to pound up into her until he threw his head back. He moaned her name, and she felt his cock pulse inside of her, pumping her full of his seed. He didn't stop thrusting, and she milked every last drop from him, squeezing him tight even as they both collapsed on the floor.

They lay there for a few minutes, not saying anything. She enjoyed the silence, actually; with her ear pressed to his chest, she could only hear his heartbeat. When he grew soft and slipped out of her, she sighed deep and rolled off him. A hand around her waist prevented her from going too far.

"Where do you think you're going?" His lips found the sensitive area on her neck and she melted back against him.

"Nowhere," she moaned.

"Damn right." His grip tightened on her and his other arm slipped underneath her. "It's been a long day." He pressed a kiss to her ear. "Let's get some rest."

She nodded and settled against him. This is what she'd

wanted, what she'd been dreaming about. To be in Zac's arms, and even if it was just for one night, to have him look at her like she was the only woman who existed. She didn't even care what tomorrow would bring. This was one memory she would cherish for the rest of her life.

CHAPTER THIRTEEN

W hen Zac woke up the next day, they were still cuddled close together, though Astrid must have shifted positions sometime in the middle of the night as her face was now pressed against his chest. For a moment, his sleep-fogged mind thought that he'd been dreaming, but the memories of last night were so clear that he knew it was real. This—having her in his arms as she slept—was real too.

She looked even more beautiful than she did last night, if that were possible. With her face so peaceful and her hair spread out behind her and over her shoulders like a golden cape, she looked perfect. Like an angel.

He didn't want to wake her or have this moment end. It still blew his mind that she'd apparently had a crush on him all these years. Of course, he was glad he didn't bump into her as a shy teenager. Seeing her at thirteen when he was seventeen would have been too weird. But what if he'd seen her when she was twenty-one, in that vintage dress she talked about? Did they waste all this time because he wanted to do his duty to his family and his clan?

It doesn't matter. What only mattered was now. His wolf wholeheartedly agreed; hell, it was practically glowing, so pleased that they had claimed her finally.

Mine. Ours.

He blinked. What did it say? Did his wolf just—

A sound from outside interrupted his thoughts. It sounded like ... digging? There were also voices. Faint, but he could hear them. When he shifted to turn his head toward the door, Astrid's eyes flew open.

"I—what the—is it—" She sat up and looked around. Her eyes widened. "I think they're here!" She shot to her feet.

Fucking hell. While he was relieved that rescue had come, couldn't they have waited another damn hour? He wanted more time with Astrid. In the daylight, her naked body was even more glorious, and he couldn't wait to have her again. With a grumble, he stood up.

"Where are your clothes?" She was already slipping the shirt she had been wearing last night over her head.

"I dried them near the fire." He walked over to the fireplace, grabbing his shirt and pants. The sound of their rescuers grew louder and he dressed hurriedly. "Here." He handed Astrid his jacket. "You should put this on."

She shook her head. "I need to head out. Before they get in here."

"What do you mean?"

"Those rescuers can't know how I got to you first," she said.

"We could say you were with me the whole time," he pointed out.

"But they've seen me at the resort. How do you think I was able to find you?"

Irritation was niggling at him. It was like she couldn't wait to get away and it was annoying the hell out of him. "We'll figure out some kind of explanation."

"But if we can't, then the Alpha will have to send my father here to use the forgetting potion and then I'll be in trouble. We both will be," she said. "Look, Zac, it's simpler this way."

He crossed his arms over his chest and stared down at her. "Simpler for who? What are you trying to—"

There was a loud pounding on the door. "Mr. Vrost! Are you in there?"

"Goddammit!" He turned his head and shouted, "Yes, I'm here!" Before he could even look back at Astrid, he heard the distinctive *poof* sound and she was gone.

Fucking hell.

He'd seen that uneasy look in her eyes, the same one she had when she wanted to avoid him. If she thought she was going to get away from him this time, she was wrong.

The door burst open, but he hardly noticed as he was already thinking about what he wanted to say to Astrid.

"Mr. Vrost!" A tall man in bright orange rescue gear stomped through the door. "Thank God we found you! Are you all right? We have an EMT outside and—"

"I'm fine," he assured him. "I just want to get back to the resort as soon as possible." Before Astrid had a chance to escape. There was a feeling in his gut that told him she would be gone by the time he got there.

"We have a couple people on snowmobiles who could give you a ride back," his rescuer said.

"Can't you get a chopper in?" He didn't mean to sound irate and demanding, but he had to beat Astrid down the mountain.

"Sorry, snow's still too fragile. A chopper could cause another avalanche. Don't worry, you can use the service route in the back and it'll get you there faster."

He mumbled a thanks and then headed out of the cabin, walking over to the first person he saw riding a snowmobile. After explaining who he was to the driver, they were soon headed down the mountain. They arrived back at the resort and the driver had barely stopped before he hopped off with a hurried thank you.

"Adrianna!" She was standing in the lobby, speaking with the two Lycan guards.

Adrianna turned her head, and when they locked eyes, her face broke into a relieved expression. "Zac! Thank God—"

"Zac!" Small arms wound around him from behind. "Oh, Zac," Isabelle cried. "I was so worried about you. I'm so glad you're okay."

"Uh, thanks." He gingerly unwound the young girl's arms from his torso and then strode over to Adrianna. He did not have the patience to deal with Isabelle now. He had to find Astrid.

"We got the call that they had found you. Are you really okay?" she asked, concern in her voice.

"Yes, I'm fine. Where's Astrid?"

"Astrid?" Adrianna asked. "She came back about thirty minutes ago. She explained that she had found you and had sought shelter in the cabin, but that she left as soon as she heard the rescuers coming to avoid any suspicion. Anyway, we're sorry we couldn't get help to you sooner. We were able to track the bracelet, but Daric and Cross were both indisposed until this morning. Cross came just as Astrid arrived."

"So, where is she?"

"They left."

His heart dropped like a heavy stone. "What do you mean they left? Which airport did they use?"

"No airport," she said. "In fact, all the runways are closed until they clear the snow. Astrid said she had some important business and asked that Cross transport her back to New York."

"And you let her go?" His voice rose a few decibels louder than he would have liked.

"Of course." Adrianna pursed her lips and narrowed her eyes at him. "Is anything the matter, Zac?"

"Nothing," he replied sharply. "When can we take off?"

"I don't know." She shrugged. "They're backed up at the airport. Possibly not until tonight."

He had a feeling tonight would be too late. There was an urgency in him to see Astrid. "There's nothing we can do?"

"I'm afraid not." She seemed resigned, and—if he read her correctly—not even the least bit angry that they would be delayed. "I guess I'll head off to my room then and get some work done." Pivoting on her heels, she headed off toward the elevators.

"If you're thinking of trying to get a flight out, don't bother," Isabelle piped up.

He didn't even realize that she was still there. "No?"

"Yeah, I tried finding a seat, but they're all booked up. I'm supposed to be back in New York tonight for a gala, but looks like I'll be missing it. And no way Adrianna's in a hurry to get back."

"She's not?"

Isabelle let out a breath. "Yeah, so I overheard her talking to Mama and Papa this morning. They want her home as soon as possible. And if I know her, she's going to try to delay that trip as long as possible."

"Why wouldn't she want to go back to New York?"

"Not New York. *Jersey.*" Isabelle's nose wrinkled delicately like she had smelled something bad. "Mama and Papa are speeding up the ascension as soon as possible. It could be in the next few weeks. Even days. And as you know, my sister's in no hurry to move back to Barnsville," she said, mentioning the name of the Lupa's hometown and the base of power for the New Jersey Lycans.

Interesting. He sympathized with Adrianna, but he

had other things on his mind right now. With seemingly no way back home until later tonight, he would just have to sit tight. Hopefully, Astrid didn't decide to move away to Timbuktu before he could make it home.

———

Apparently, Adrianna had been so reluctant to go back home that she instructed the pilot to take the last possible takeoff time. She said it was so they wouldn't have to be stuck inside the jet, but it was frustrating to say the least.

Every moment Zac was away from Astrid made him anxious. It was maddening and confusing, but she had been so eager to get away from him that he just knew something was wrong. He would have walked all the way to New York if he could; hell, his own inner wolf was pushing him to leave. But he had no choice.

They arrived in New York at around four in the morning. He hurried back to his hotel room, got showered, dressed, and headed to Fenrir as soon as he could. There was a lot of work waiting for him, and he finished as soon as he could, speeding through conference calls and barely reading his emails. By mid-morning, he was finally headed down to the fifteenth floor to find Astrid.

The trainees were already doing their exercises by the time he got there, jogging around the room. Meredith and Nick were at the front, directing them. Zac's eyes immediately zeroed in on Astrid, and he was relieved to see she hadn't left New York. She must have felt his eyes on her because she turned her head and their eyes locked. Her cheeks went all pink, then she stumbled forward and the woman at her back smacked right into her.

"Jonasson," the woman grumbled. "Watch where you're going."

"Wha—oh, sorry!" She straightened herself, keeping her gaze straight ahead and avoiding his as she went back to her place in line.

A prickle ran over the back of his neck and he knew someone was watching him. It was his father, and his ice blue eyes pierced right into him. Nick whispered something to Meredith and handed her the clipboard in his hands, then made his way toward him.

"Zac," he began. "I didn't think you'd be coming in today."

"I told you and Mom I was fine." He had spoken with his parents yesterday to assure them he was all right.

"I know," Nick said. "But why are you here? I mean, I appreciate that you seem to be taking an interest in the security team, but don't you have work at the office as well?"

"I do," he said. "But I thought I'd drop in for a while and see the progress the trainees were making."

"I see." Nick straightened his shoulders. "You're welcome to stay, of course, but perhaps you should see your mother. She was worried sick about you. She won't rest easy until she's seen you."

Was his father trying to make him leave? He searched Nick's face to see if he had suspected anything, but as always, he put on that cold facade that gave nothing away. "I'll make sure to drop in then."

"See that you do." Nick turned on his heel and went back to the front of the room. He said a few words to Meredith, to which she nodded and then blew on the whistle around her neck.

"All right trainees," she shouted. "Now for a little endurance test. We're going to keep jogging for another hour. No breaks."

There were groans and murmurs from amongst the trainees, but when Meredith blew on the whistle, everyone trudged back into line and started jogging again.

Zac clenched his jaw. He supposed he could stay here another hour until they finished, but the steely, challenging gaze his father sent him made him think that if he did, the trainees would have an added hour of jogging time. Nick Vrost was too damn perceptive for his own good.

He conceded defeat for now, walked out of the training room, and headed up to the executive floors. His mother practically mauled him when he walked into her office, and he tried to calm her down.

"I'm right here, Mom," he said. "See? I'm all right."

"Oh, Zac, when they told me ..." Cady's voice broke and tears pooled in her eyes. "I just ... I'm your mother, you know? I'll never stop worrying about you."

"I know," he said quietly. "I promise never to put you through that again."

They chatted for a few more minutes and made plans to have lunch together before he headed off to his own temporary office. He busied himself with work for the rest of the day, but in the back of his mind he planned his strategy to get Astrid alone again so they could talk about what happened. He decided he would wait until the end of the day, when his father and mother went home.

As soon as the clock on his desk read 6:00 p.m., he stood up and made his way to the private elevators. He punched the number for the sixteenth floor. Hopefully this time, he wouldn't have to trap Astrid in the broom closet again. As luck would have it, as soon as the door opened, she was standing right in front of him, dressed in her street clothes, obviously about to head out.

"Zac! What are you—hey!"

He didn't want to lose her again, so he grabbed her arm. "Which is your room?" he asked.

"My what?"

"Your room," he repeated. "Unless you want a repeat of what happened in the broom closet?"

"I—" Her pink cheeks puffed out and she gestured toward the hallway lined with doors. "Third on the left."

He swiftly dragged her down, opened the door and shoved her inside. "Now," he turned around, "tell me why you ran away."

"I told you why." She looked away from him, as if the empty wall suddenly looked like the most interesting thing in the world. "I didn't want to raise any suspicion and—"

"Don't give me that bullshit, Astrid." He took a step forward, making her stagger back. Refusing to let her get another inch away from him, he tugged at her sleeve to pull her to him. "You didn't have to put an entire country between us. We need to talk."

"I don't expect anything from you." She looked up at him with a defiant stare. "There's no need to make this anymore awkward. I thought we agreed that what happened in the cabin would stay there."

"I didn't agree to anything." He spanned his hands around her slim waist, moving around to rest on the small of her back. "I wanted you then, Astrid. And I still want you now."

She turned away from him when he leaned down to kiss her, his lips landed on a cool cheek. "Please. Zac."

He was not going to give up. Trailing his lips down to her neck, he licked at that soft spot just behind her earlobe. "Please *what*, Astrid?" He could smell her arousal even now, and as if to prove his point, he pressed his erection against her hip.

She moaned and twisted her head up to face him. "I want you, too. Kiss me again."

He didn't need to be asked twice. Bending his head down, he captured her mouth, drinking from her as if he'd been parched for years and the only way to quench his thirst was her. She gave just as good, her tongue snaking into his mouth hungrily, coaxing him and asking for more.

Her hands landed on his chest and she pushed him back. Complying, he stepped backwards until the backs of his knees hit the edge of something. When she pushed him down, he realized that he was sitting on her bed. He shook off his suit jacket and loosened his tie.

Amber eyes blazed with desire as she stared down at him, and she began to strip. First, her shoes, then her leggings along with her underwear and then off came her shirt. She reached behind to unhook her lacy bra and in no time, she was standing between his knees, wearing only a smile.

He looked up at her in awe. Did she know how gorgeous she was? The first time she bared her body to him was a sight that had been burned into his brain. Her skin glowing in the firelight. Her hair like gold. She looked like a sensual goddess. Even now, she was still as beautiful, and he ached to have her and be inside her again.

She got on her knees on the floor as he was unbuttoning his shirt. When she reached for his belt buckle, he saw her hands shake, but she freed him from the confines of what was left of his clothing. He was already hard, of course, but her soft palm around his cock made him even more rigid. She stroked him, tentatively at first, her head lifting to meet his gaze as she leaned forward.

"Astrid, you don't—argh!" He bit his lip as her wet mouth engulfed his tip. She closed her eyes briefly, as if savoring him, but opened them again to look up at him. Her head bobbed forward and back, sending his pleasure centers into overdrive. *Jesus.* Seeing her pink, plump lips wrapped around his cock was the hottest fucking thing he had ever seen and he nearly lost control.

He dug his fingers into her hair and pulled back gently. "I'm not gonna last long if you keep that up."

With a nod, she released him, but crawled up to the

bed, forcing him to move back. She placed her hands on his shoulders to push him down so he was prone on the mattress. Straddling his hips, she reached down to wrap her hand around his cock again and guided the tip into her entrance.

"Fuck. Astrid!" He changed his mind; *this* was the hottest fucking thing he'd ever seen. Astrid over him, taking his cock inside her, sinking down on him. She flinched when he was fully inside her, but after a few moments, she sighed with pleasure.

Engulfed in her warmth and wetness, he never wanted this moment to end. Then, she began to move, her hips grinding back and forth in small motions. His greedy eyes devoured every inch of her, from her gorgeous face thrown back in pleasure, down to her delicate collarbones, to her breasts bouncing up and down as she increased her movements, and lower still over the smooth skin of her flat belly to the light thatch of blonde hair between her legs.

She moaned, shifting her hips and clenching him tighter. He reached down between them to find her wet, hardened clit, plucking at the bud until she was crying out in pleasure. "Zac!" His name on her lips as she came hard was the sweetest thing he'd ever heard, and he pumped his hips up seeking more of her. When she slowed down her hips, he took the opportunity to flip her over so he was on top.

He got on his knees and hauled her to him, pushing inside her again, filling her. She yelped, her eyes opening in surprise. He fucked into her, hard and fast, hooking an arm under one leg to keep her in place. Her back arched up as he continued to pummel into her, and she cried out, clawing at his arms as her body squeezed him tight.

He leaned down to cover her body, pulling her close so her breasts pressed up against his chest. Not wanting the moment to end, he slowed down, savoring the feeling of her tight passage around him, the friction making him groan. Her fingers locked around his neck and pulled him down for a passionate kiss, her lips moving against his in a rhythm that matched their lovemaking. He couldn't contain himself, and he spilled his cum inside her, the pleasure zinging straight down his spine as she squeezed tight around him, making him shudder and groan against her mouth. He didn't release her lips, wanting more of her sweetness like he couldn't get enough.

Rolling them over so she was on top, she was the one who lifted her head to break their kiss. Letting out a sigh, she relaxed against him, laying her cheek on his chest.

They lay there in silence for a few minutes. He didn't want to say anything, he didn't even want to move or breathe for fear that she might just disappear like smoke again.

"You seem so serious." She had her hands crossed over his chest and propped her chin up over her fingers. "What are you thinking of?"

"Nothing important." He reached down to brush a lock of hair that had stuck to her forehead. "What are you thinking of?"

She smirked at him. "How unfair it is."

"Unfair?"

"How am I supposed to sneak out when you corner me in my own room?"

A snarl ripped from his throat and he rolled her over, trapping her with his body. "Here's the answer: you *don't*." He kissed her, perhaps a little too forcefully, but her words made him furious. "You're mine, Astrid. And you're not getting away from me." No, never again. He was not letting go of her. Ever.

CHAPTER FOURTEEN

Astrid had never slept so soundly as she did that night, but then again, she'd never been so exhausted. Zac kept her up most of the night, only stopping because she was starving after their fourth round, and he let her go to the cafeteria to get some snacks. He was relentless the rest of the night and by her seventh orgasm, she basically stopped counting, and it was around midnight she begged him to let her close her eyes. She was out cold within minutes.

That's probably why the very loud ringing coming from somewhere on the floor didn't wake her at first. It was only when she felt the bed shift and she lost the warmth of his body did she open her eyes.

"Zac?" She rubbed the sleep from her eyes and found him standing with his back to her, his tight ass on display for her to admire. *What I wouldn't give to have a quarter right now*, she thought. Hell, silver dollars could bounce off Zac's buns ....

"... And you really can't get anyone else?" Zac's body tensed, then he let out a breath. "Fine. Book me on the first flight out." He put the phone down on the bedside table and turned to face her. He looked thoroughly annoyed.

"What's wrong?"

"Trouble at the London office." He scratched his head seemingly unaware he was completely naked and sporting a half-chubby. "I need to head over there."

She stretched out like a cat and yawned. "Well, if you have to—Zac!" She giggled when he swooped down on the bed and tackled her from behind.

"You are making it very hard for me to get on that plane," he whispered in her ear.

"That," she rubbed her ass on his now-hardening cock, "is the point, Zachary. Oh!" She moaned when his fingers slipped between her legs. He teased her until she was soaking and then nudged her thighs apart with his knees, and her eyes rolled back when he entered her in one swift motion.

He held her tight, one arm around her waist and the other over her breasts as he fucked her from behind. This morning's sex session was quick and rough, and as soon as her body tightened around him, he let out a guttural sound, and she felt his cock twitch inside her as he came. Their movements slowed down and they lay there, panting as their breathing returned to normal.

"I'm sorry," he said. "I really do have to leave."

After their time in Colorado, she was the one who had run from him, unable to face the reality of what they had done. Or perhaps she wanted to be the first one to pull away before she got hurt. Last night, she couldn't believe he would come after her, especially after she'd been too much of a coward to face him. And now, he was the one leaving.

"I'm not running away."

She stiffened. It was like he could read her mind. "I didn't say that."

"I know, but," he kissed her neck, "I just wanted to let you know. I'm not leaving you forever, not by a long shot. If I could, I'd bring you with me."

"The terms of my punishment wouldn't allow me to just take a vacation," she said.

"I'll be back as soon as I can. A few days, tops," he promised. "I really do hate to leave, but ..."

She twisted her body to face him, then lifted her head up to place a kiss on his lips. "You have your thing. This is your thing and I have mine. Just ... keep in touch."

"I will." He kissed her, long and deep, and even as he tried to rise form the bed, she sat up with him, not quite ready to let him go. "We'll talk when I get back."

She swallowed the lump in her throat. "Right." She glanced at the clock. It was four o'clock in the morning, so it should be safe for him to leave. Safe? Well, they didn't talk about what they were exactly, but still, it probably wouldn't be a good thing if anyone saw the Beta's son doing the walk of shame out of her room.

As he dressed, she lay back in bed, gathering the covers around her. When he finished, she stood up to walk him to the door. "Have a safe flight," she said.

He caressed her cheek with his fingers. "I will." Leaning down, he brushed his lips over hers softly. She didn't move, didn't breathe, didn't even open her eyes when his lips left hers. And when she did open them, he was gone.

———

If it wasn't for Zac's lingering scent, she would have thought she'd gone crazy and hallucinated all of what happened. Her heart ached the entire morning, feeling so empty knowing that Zac was three thousand miles away from her. She went through the motions of her morning training, going to lunch, and the afternoon's learning sessions.

It was around three o'clock when she got a message from an unknown London number during their afternoon break time. She was sitting down, having a cup of coffee and some muffins in the kitchen with some of the other trainees when her phone beeped.

Hi, beautiful. Made it back in one piece.

Her heart skipped a beat at the words on the tiny screen. She glanced around her, wondering if any of the people next to her could see the big grin on her face. Looking back down at her phone, an evil thought popped into her head.

Who's this?

She pressed send and waited for his reply. It came back in no time.

That guy who snuck into your room and gave you ten orgasms. <Licking emoji>

She snorted loudly, which made hot coffee stream down from her nose and splatter her shirt. That got the attention of Layla, who was sitting beside her. She arched a dark brow at her but said nothing. Astrid fumed and typed out a message with one finger as she mopped herself up with a napkin.

Justin???? Send.

She hadn't even had a chance to toss the sodden napkin when her phone starting ringing.

"Who the *hell* is Justin?" came Zac's angry voice.

"Oh, boo." She held the phone to her ear with her shoulders as she washed her hand. Everyone had left the break room, so she deemed it safe to talk. "That was payback."

"Are you mad I left?"

"What? No." She denied emphatically. "That last text you sent made me snort coffee through my nose and now my shirt's all stained with coffee."

He chuckled. "Sweetheart, I hate to break it to you, but half your shirts are stained with coffee."

True, but that wasn't the point. "How was the flight?"

"Boring. Long." There was the sound of something rustling in the background. "Sorry, just unwrapping my sandwich. Didn't have much time to eat. I was working most of the flight here. How was your day?"

"Same old, same old." She leaned back against the sink. "Did you—"

"Yo, Jonasson! Stop sexting with your boyfriend." Layla popped her head in through the break room door. "Get your butt downstairs! Your old lady's about to have an aneurysm."

"Sorry, *Justin*," she said with a laugh. "I'll talk to you later."

"Until later."

For the rest of the week, they communicated mainly through text during the day. He was five hours ahead, so she would always wake up to a very sweet good morning text from him, as well as details of how his morning went. She would text him during her breaks, about how training was going and by the time she was done, he was already winding down and they would continue texting as she was having dinner. Two days after he left, she convinced him to stay up past his bedtime for a naughty chat session, though ultimately, it left both of them unsatisfied.

She couldn't bring herself to ask him when he was coming back. It sounded too needy on her end. She was aching to be near him. He didn't supply the information anyway, but from what he'd been telling her, there really was a major problem at the London office. Then, on Thursday, he had to fly to Estonia which made the time difference even more difficult.

When Friday rolled around, she got her usual morning

messages, but his responses to her texts took longer and longer to arrive. When he didn't respond right away, she tried everything from shutting her phone off and checking if the Internet in the building was working. By evening, she said goodnight to him, but didn't even get a response back.

"He's probably sleeping," she told herself as she sat in her room after dinner. It was two o'clock in the morning in Estonia, after all. The rest of the trainees invited her to go out to Blood Moon, but she declined. She wanted to be in her room, just in case Zac called.

She fell asleep reading the latest trashy romance novel from her favorite author and the next day, she woke up with her e-reader in her hand. Her stomach gurgled. God, these training sessions were so brutal, she was famished all day long. This entire week, she had at least three plates for breakfast, lunch, and dinner. Despite her tummy's demands to be filled right this moment, she realized that she hadn't checked her phone yet.

Her heart soared when she saw the message notification. Her finger tapped on the screen.

Hey.

"Hey?" she said aloud. Twelve hours of radio silence and all he could say was "hey"? She wanted to toss the phone across the room, but decided she could play this game too.

Hey. Send.

He replied faster this time. *Have you had breakfast yet?*

Her stomach growled loudly. Breakfast was definitely in order. She was scrounging around for that package of cookies she kept somewhere in her closet when her phone beeped again.

That bagel place around the corner should have just opened.

Hmmm. Fresh bagels with a schmear of cream cheese and some lox and capers sounded great right about now. Her stomach agreed. She decided that Zac could wait and she needed food *now*, so she threw on some sweats, her coat, boots, and headed downstairs.

As she rode the elevator down, she stared at her phone, wondering what to write back. She wanted to sound casual, but not *too* casual in case it made her sound like she was being apathetic. But then again, she didn't want to seem needy or dramatic either. *Ugh.*

All week long, they had been texting non-stop. Sometimes the messages were sweet, other times spicy. Or just typical banter. Once in a while he would say something that made her heart belly-flop right into her stomach. Like when he was describing the view of the Thames from his apartment and wished she was there with him. Or that sexy morning selfie he took the other day, with his hair mussed ...

When she reached the lobby, she still hadn't sent him anything and her fingers hovered nervously over the screen. She walked out the door of the building, biting her lip as she racked her brain, trying to find the right words to say. She was so engrossed that she didn't hear the voice calling her right away.

"Astrid. *Astrid.*"

She was so surprised that she dropped her phone on the sidewalk, and it bounced on the pavement, skidding a few feet from her. She cursed and bent down to pick it up. *Thank God for protective cases.* When she looked up, she saw Zac, leaning casually against his Porsche, grinning at her.

"Z-zac!" Her feet seemingly had a life of their own as she sped toward him, running straight into his arms. God, this felt so good, feeling his body against hers. He lifted her up in a tight hug and pressed his lips to hers.

"You taste even better than I remembered," he said when he pulled away.

"I was beginning to think you'd forgotten about me."

"Forget you? Never." He kissed her nose and put her down on her feet. "Sorry for not answering you back, but I've been traveling for about twenty hours now."

"Twenty hours?" she asked. "Why the hell would it take nearly a day to get back to New York from London?"

He let out a long sigh. "I made the mistake of hitching a ride with Bastian."

She chuckled. "Ah, I think I understand." Sebastian "Bastian" Creed Jr., one of Deedee's brothers, was the typical playboy billionaire, jetting off all over the world. His biotech company had blown up in the last couple of years, and so he spent most of his time traveling the world and always seemed to be photographed at glamorous parties with A-list celebrities.

"I saw him in Tallin where he was showing off his latest software acquisition. He said he was heading back to

New York in his private jet and that I should join him." His brows furrowed together. "In the middle of the flight, he told his pilot to stop in Ibiza for a drink, and then one drink turned into two, and then—"

"You don't have to tell me." She knew all about Bastian Creed's partying ways, at least from Deedee and Aunt Jade's stories. "Did you end up in a hot tub full of lime jello with Spanish supermodels?"

"It was strawberry and they were Russian." When her lips thinned with annoyance, he laughed and kissed her. "I'm joking," he said. "But I fooled you there for a moment."

"You wish." When she struggled to get away from him, he held her tighter.

"C'mon." He nodded to his car. "Let's go for a ride."

"Are you taking me to breakfast?"

Opening the passenger door, he gestured to the brown paper bag sitting on the dash. "I already got you breakfast."

"Ooohhh!" She slipped inside the car and snatched the bag. "Still warm."

He closed the door and walked around to the driver's side. She was already stuffing her mouth when he sat down.   "This—yummmmm—is—grrrmmm—delicious." The cinnamon raisin bagel was so fresh and the cream cheese added just the right amount of salty-savory flavor. She swallowed the whole bite, and though her stomach demanded more, she put the bagel down on her lap and turned to him. "Wait, did you just lure me into your car with *food*?"

He laughed and stepped on the gas. "It worked, right?"

"Oh my God! You're kidnapping me."

When he stopped at a red light, he reached over to wipe a bit of cream cheese from the corner of her mouth. "Sweetheart." He licked his thumb, making her mouth go dry when she saw his tongue dart out of his mouth. "I just want us to be alone for the weekend."

"Weekend?" she asked in an incredulous voice. "We're going away for the weekend?"

"Yes."

"B-b-but I don't have any clothes packed." Oh God, why hadn't she thrown on something—anything—nicer than her Mickey Mouse sweats and her ratty old coat?

The light turned green and he looked ahead. "We can stop somewhere and get you some basics. But you won't be needing clothes where we're going." His gaze flickered toward her, full of heat and promise. She couldn't help her body's reaction—her breath catching and her core clenching with need as her panties flooded with arousal. That seemed to amuse him more as his lips curled up into a smile.

She leaned back and stared down at the partially-eaten bagel. *I guess we're going away for the weekend.*

CHAPTER FIFTEEN

A s Zac promised, they stopped by a big box store on the way to wherever the hell they were going. Astrid would have thought that a surprise weekend getaway was romantic, except A, she didn't even have enough money on her to buy her own clothes—which meant he paid for everything—and B, he seemed to revel in the idea that she was completely in the dark about the whole thing.

"Are you still mad at me?" he asked as they got back into the car.

"I'm still deciding." She reached over to the radio and flipped on the dial.

"*And in world news,*" the female newscaster's voice burst through the speakers, "*it is with deepest sadness we announce that His Majesty, King Nassir Assam Sala-muddin of Zhobgahdi has passed away at the age of eighty. We are awaiting an official statement from the Royal Palace*

—" The volume made her cringe, so she reached over and turned the dial down. "Are you going to tell me where we're going?"

"I don't know, you look too cute when you're mad," he teased.

"Too cute—Oh you shithead!" She slapped him lightly on the arm and laughed. "Just drive." She supposed that she would find out soon enough anyway.

About two hours later, they arrived in Upstate New York. The road they drove on followed the Hudson River, and on this perfect winter morning, the Hudson Valley looked absolutely stunning. She looked at Zac, but he seemed to be concentrated on driving. After a few more miles, he pulled into a smaller road, then turned off into a driveway before stopping in front of a large gate. He pressed a button on his car's dash and the gates swung open.

The driveway was long and sprawling, but it didn't take long until they reached the house. Well, to call it a house would have been an insult. It was more like a mansion, huge and imposing, but somehow, welcoming at the same time. There were four large columns with a triangular top in front that gave it a stately facade. Arched windows, cornices, and a large tower-like structure on the south side. It was like one of those stately manors from those old movies and she half-expected some 1920s, monocle-wearing, cigar-chomping robber baron to walk out.

He stopped the car in front of the driveway, exited, and walked over to open the door for her.

"Zac ... what is this place?" She looked up in wonder as she took his hand as he helped her out.

"This is my home," he said.

"You ... own this?" Her mind was reeling.

"Yes," he said. "Well, it originally belonged to my great-grandfather, Vasili Vrost."

"Oh. I think I remember him." She recalled seeing an older man who looked similar to Nick at a couple of Lycan events when she was growing up. Then it struck her. He said it belonged to his great-grandfather. Past tense. "Wait, is he ..."

"Five years ago," he finished.

There was a sadness that passed across his face briefly and her heart ached for him. She squeezed his hand. "So, he left you this entire mansion?"

"Not quite. Technically, all his properties, business, and other assets went to my father, which would have been divided between my siblings and I," he explained. He took a key from his pocket and opened the front door. The interior was even more stunning, opening up to a spacious, airy foyer that led up to a grand staircase. Various paintings covered the wall and the decor and furniture looked original. The carpet on the floor looked Persian and very expensive.

"But, with Vasili gone, he knew that none of us would have had time to come here anyway. He thought about selling the place, but he just couldn't. So, a year ago, I offered to buy out my sibling's shares. They were only too happy to let me have it, if only to keep it in the family. I've mostly left it the way it was, the way my great-grandmother had it decorated when Vasili bought it for her."

"It's beautiful," she said. "I'm glad you were able to keep it the way it was."

"It would have been his wish."

She wanted to know more about his great-grandfather, but she could sense the mood changing. She only had one grandparent who was still alive—her grandmother Signe, who lived with the New York Coven. Though she wasn't particularly close to Signe, she couldn't imagine what it would be like to lose her.

"Zac." She wove her fingers through his. "Why don't you give me a tour later and for now ... just show me the bedroom?"

His expression changed. There was that flash of desire in his eyes that she knew so well. "Happily," he said, as he led her up the stairs.

———

After a lazy morning spent in bed, they drove out to the town to have lunch and then pick up some supplies for dinner at the general store. "Ooh, I'm going to need some snacks, too!" Astrid declared as they passed a bakery. "Oh my God, that smells amazing."

When she left the bakery armed with two paper bags, he gave her a curious look.

"You owe me for kidnapping me in my sweats," she

said. To which he replied with a laugh and a kiss on the nose.

Although Zac had kept the mansion as it had been when he was growing up, he explained to Astrid that he did add a few modern conveniences, including the hot tub that he had installed on the balcony of the master bedroom. As soon as they came back, they took a dip.

"Oohhhh," she sighed as she eased down into the hot water. "This feels so good."

"I'm sorry if I've made you too sore," he said.

She splashed some water at his face. "The look on your face says you're not sorry at all." He laughed and then pulled her to his lap.

She relaxed against him and looked out to the spectacular view of the Hudson river and the valley. The trees, except for the evergreen ones, were bare and the hills covered in snow. There was that hush quiet atmosphere that could only happen in the winter time. "It's beautiful out here," she said. "I can see why you wanted to keep this place."

"I spent a lot of time here as a child." He rested his chin on her shoulder. "All Christmases, of course, and a couple summers."

"You ... you were close with Vasili?"

"Yes."

He seemed to only answer in single syllables when she asked about his great-grandfather, so she decided to move away from the subject for now. "Are there people who look out for the place while you're away?"

"Yeah, I have a management company come in and do the cleaning and maintenance. This is actually only the second time I've come here since I bought it."

"It must have taken an army of servants to run this place during your great-grandfather's time," she said.

"Not really. There were some maids and a cook, plus we had Garret."

"What's a Garret?"

His lips turned up into a fond smile. "Vasili's most trusted servant," he said. "He was an old-school butler who served my great-grandfather for decades. He was stern and ran this house like a captain on a navy boat. But he was also very kind and great at a lot things like sewing and baking."

"Really?"

"Yeah." There was that sad expression on his face again. "He died not long after my grandfather."

"I'm so sorry, Zac." She turned to face him, straddling his lap. "About Vasili and Garret."

"He lived to a hundred years old," he said. "He was a stubborn old man. Both of them were. But it was just their time."

She reached up to cup his face. "That doesn't make it hurt any less. It's okay to still be sad, you know, after all this time. Just because you're a guy, doesn't mean you're not allowed to mourn and be sad when you think of him."

He swallowed, his Adam's apple bobbing up and down. "I know."

"Besides," she said. "You must have had a lot of great memories with him and Garret."

"Definitely." His face lit up. "There was this one Christmas, I was probably five or six. I was definitely old enough to remember for sure. Anyway, Vasili had hired someone to play Santa on Christmas morning for me and my siblings, but he didn't show up. Not wanting to disappoint any of us, Garret volunteered to play Santa."

"And then what happened?"

"I didn't witness this, of course, but my mother told me the story. Santa actors provide their own suits, right? They didn't know how to get one on Christmas Eve. So, he and Garret stayed up all night trying to put together a last-minute Santa outfit. They borrowed one of my mother's robes and then sewed cotton balls all around it for the fur and for the fake beard. They found some old belts in the attic that belonged to my great-grandmother."

"That must have been a sight," she laughed.

"Yeah. But it was the best Santa I'd ever seen." There was a flash of joy in his eyes, which then quickly turned dark, and his body suddenly went rigid.

A sadness wrapped around her, and it was like she could feel the pain in his heart. "He must have loved you." She stroked her fingers through his hair as she looked straight into his eyes. "I'm sorry, I'm making you sad."

"No, don't be sorry." His breath hitched and he cast his eyes downward. "It's nice ... remembering the good times. I just haven't had time to think of them lately. Not when all I can think about is how he's gone."

"But he's not truly gone." Sliding her hand down, she placed her palm over his heart. "He's right here. He's here in all of you. Your siblings, your parents, and everyone that remembers him. He'll also live on because of you and what you did to keep the house in your family."

He paused, then lifted his head up. "Thank you," he said. "You've given me a lot to think about."

"I did? What about?"

"I'm not sure yet. But when I do, I'll let you know. Now." The intensity in his ice blue eyes made heat shoot through her body. "I think it's time we get down to the real reason I kidnapped you."

"Kidnapped me? You mean, to your gorgeous mansion and your hot tub?" She let out a laugh. "You're free to kidnap me any time. In fact, if you have an apartment in Paris, you can kidnap me—"

He silenced her with his lips, pressing his mouth to hers and sending a shockwave through her body. She moaned aloud when his fingers slipped between her thighs underneath the roiling hot water, caressing her and making her body shudder. "Yes," she sighed when his mouth moved lower, tracing a scorching path down to the valley between her breasts. *I could get used to this,* she thought as his head dipped below the water.

CHAPTER SIXTEEN

Zac never hated Sunday night more than he did now. He didn't want the weekend to end and have to face reality on Monday morning. He tried to convince Astrid to stay one more night, but she wouldn't relent.

"I can't show up in the morning fresh from a weekend getaway," she had said. Besides, although she was free to come and go as she pleased in her own time, the trainees did have a curfew on Sunday nights.

And so, he relented, packing up the car on Sunday afternoon so they could be back in New York by evening. He was, at least, able to coax her to come up to his room for dinner. And by dinner, he meant more sex and an enormous room service order that took two bellmen to deliver.

She had to be back in her room by midnight, so at around eleven o'clock, they said their goodbyes. While she declined his offer of a ride, she did let him call her an

Uber. They also made plans to meet at the ramen restaurant on Fortieth and Lexington for dinner the following night.

On Monday morning, he went back to work and it took all his willpower not to stop by the sixteenth floor just to see Astrid. As he tried to concentrate on his emails, his thoughts kept going back to the glorious weekend they had.

The whole week he was away from her had been torture, not to mention the fact that he still didn't know what the hell was going on. What were they to each other? He'd made up conversations in his mind, trying to bring up the subject, but when he finally was in front of her, he never even brought it up. It was like he couldn't think of anything, and everything else seemed trivial. His inner wolf seemed to know something, but what, he couldn't tell. All he knew was that the animal was happier and content around her.

Besides, he wanted to keep Astrid to himself for a while longer. Having to come out and give themselves a label seemed to cheapen what they had. Whatever it was, he didn't have a name for it.

Then, there was the subject of his father. There was that niggling feeling in his brain that something wasn't quite right. He racked his brain, trying to figure out a way to talk to Nick and tell him about Astrid. What should he say? Or expect his father's reaction to be?

Of course, he didn't expect the man himself to show up at his office at that moment.

"Dad?" He looked up from his computer as Nick

strode into the room, an inscrutable look on his face. He closed the door behind him and locked it.

"No need to stand up," Nick said. "I'll be quick."

He frowned, but sat back down. "What can I do for you, Dad?"

Nick marched to the front of his desk and crossed his arms over his desk, his gaze looking straight down at him. "Explain to me what you've been doing with that girl."

"What girl?"

"You *know* who I mean." Nick's jaw tensed as he took something out of his pocket. He touched the screen and then pointed the screen at him. It was video surveillance footage from the elevator lobby on the sixteenth floor. It showed him the night after Vail, when he dragged Astrid back to her room. The video switched to the morning after, when he was leaving.

Zac tamped down the anger threatening to explode from him. "I don't have to explain myself to you. Besides, are you spying on me?"

"Spying? I'm doing my job, as the head of the security team, as Beta, and as your father." His face was completely red now. "Are you sleeping with her?"

He shot to his feet. "That's none of your damn business!"

"Goddammit, Zac!" He raked his fingers through his hair. "Why *her*? Out of all the people you'd choose to fuck, why her? Is it just the sex?"

"I would choose your next words carefully," Zac warned in a soft, but deadly voice.

Nick's expression faltered. "So, it's not just sex." He rubbed a hand down his face. "I would almost prefer if it was."

"Dad," he said through gritted teeth. "Why do you hate her so much? So what if she's not one of the ruling families or she's not well-connected? Is it because Meredith works for you and used to be one of the Lone Wolves?"

"Christ!" Nick slammed his hands down on the desk. "It's not Meredith that I have a problem with. It's that Goddamn warlock! I wish to God he'd never ..."

"Daric? Dad, that's preposterous. The war between the magical beings and Lycans is over. And Daric is one of the most trusted members of the clan."

"Yes, but you don't know the truth." Nick sighed. "Sit down."

"I will not—"

"Sit down, Zachary."

The graveness in his father's voice made him sit. "Explain."

Nick took a long, deep breath. "A long time ago, we—meaning Grant, Frankie, Daric, Meredith, your mother and I—made a decision to keep certain details regarding our war with the mages out of the official records of our history. One of those details involved Daric."

"What is it?"

"Daric wasn't just some warlock who came out of nowhere to help the Lycans. He was one of them."

"Them?"

"He worked for the mages."

"What?" Coldness froze the blood in his veins and his head felt light. "I don't understand."

"We had captured him in one of the earlier battles and turned him to our side. But before that, he was the master mage Stefan's right-hand man. At one point, he kidnapped your mother."

"He what?" *Oh no.*

"They made it seem like Cady betrayed us and then kidnapped her. They wanted your mother because of her powerful witch heritage. Stefan had a plan. Daric and she would start breeding a new generation of witches."

"Breeding—" The bile rising in his throat made him stop. "Did they ..."

"No, thank God. We stopped them in time."

Zac gripped the edge of the table. His mind was reeling, and all he could think about was his poor mother. Being kidnapped and having her kidnapper—"Why did you keep this from me?"

"Because at that time, we all thought it was best," Nick said. "That we just forget about the past and move forward. Daric had pledged to us. It turns out he was being coerced into serving Stefan because the master mage had kidnapped his mother."

"So, he didn't want to help Stefan?"

"No," Nick conceded. "But I know if my own mother had been held prisoner, I would have done everything I could to keep her safe."

Zac felt all the blood from his face drain. He couldn't believe it. Did Astrid know?

"So, you see why you can't see her anymore," Nick said. He stood up and buttoned up his suit. "I'm going to your mother's office. See you later, Son."

The sound of the door slamming shut felt ominous and final. Processing this whole thing seemed impossible. His emotions were churning and he didn't know what to do.

Astrid. His mother. Daric. If this was all true—and why would his father lie?—then this was all going to be a big mess. He was loyal to his family of course, but Astrid ... he just couldn't imagine not being with her. But then again, his poor mother. What would she think? How would she feel? He couldn't break her heart like that. Family. Blood. Loyalty. Vasili Vrost and Nick had taught him that nothing else mattered.

He stood up and closed his computer, then walked out the door, stopping by the desk of the Lycan assistant assigned to him. "Jane," he said to the young woman. "Cancel all my meetings for today. I won't be coming back." He didn't bother for her reply as he headed straight for the elevators.

CHAPTER SEVENTEEN

Astrid checked her phone for what seemed like the millionth time that night. She was pretty sure she and Zac had agreed on seven-thirty for dinner at the ramen place, but thirty minutes after she'd arrived, he still wasn't here. The hostess said she couldn't seat her without everyone in their party there, even if it was just two people.

So, she waited. It was getting so crowded inside that she was pushed out to the storm door and soon found herself outside in the freezing rain. Pulling the hood of her jacket over her head, she glanced at the phone in her hand again. Zac was now an hour late.

Did something come up? Was he tied up in a meeting? Or maybe she got the address wrong. How many ramen restaurants were there on Lexington Avenue?

"Astrid."

The heaviness in her chest lifted when she heard his

voice. She whipped around so fast, her hood drew back. "Zac!" She wrapped her arms around him. "Oh, Zac. Are you okay? Did something happen?" He remained stiff with his hands at his sides. "Baby, you're all wet. Did you walk all the way here?"

"I've been walking all day."

She raised her head to stare up at his face. His expression was tense and his mouth was pulled into a thin line. "Why?"

"I just—" He removed her arms from him and set them at her sides. "We need to talk, Astrid."

"Of course. Let's go inside." She tried to take his hand, but he pulled it away. "Zac?"

"No. I mean, we can talk out here."

"It's raining."

"Please, Astrid. I can't." He turned his back to her.

What the hell was going on? She sidestepped to face him. "Zac. Talk to me."

His eyes turned hard, like shards of blue steel. "My father found out about us."

It was bound to happen, she supposed. "What did he say?"

"He wasn't happy."

"Oh." Of course not. She knew Nick would have never approved of her for his golden boy after all. Wasn't that what she'd feared all along?

"Did you know what your father was, before he came to pledge to the New York clan?"

The question came out of left field and left her

stunned for a few seconds. "My father? What does he have to do with any of this?"

"My father told me that Daric worked with the mages before he switched sides."

Her knees buckled, but she caught herself before she fell forward. "No. That's not true."

"Why would he lie?" Zac accused.

"I didn't know! I swear, Zac, I—"

"They lied to us," he said. "They lied to all of us."

"Then why are you mad at me?" she asked.

"I'm not mad at you, Astrid," he said. "But ... you need to ask your father about it. And what he tried to do to my mother."

"What he tried to—Zac, please!" She grabbed at his sleeves. "Just tell me what's going on?" It felt like she had stepped into another dimension, or a play where she didn't know her lines. Her world was turning upside down right before her very eyes.

"I'm sorry, Astrid. I just ... I can't do this. Not to her."

"Zac, I'm sure we could—please! Don't go. You said ... you said I was yours. And that you would never—"

He pulled her hands off him. "Goodbye, Astrid."

No! Her mind screamed the words. Her wolf was howling in pain, the sound so deafening she couldn't hear anything else. Not the rain as it fell harder, soaking her through her jacket. Not the cabs as the honked their horns when they passed by. Not even the people who stopped and asked her if she was okay.

No, she couldn't hear any of them as she watched Zac walk away from her like she meant nothing to him.

———

The temperatures in New York city didn't dip low enough to turn the rain into snow, so the city was pounded with freezing rain for most of the night. Astrid wasn't sure how long she walked in the cold, but she could hardly keep track of the time. Her body was numb and she allowed her legs to lead the way. Perhaps something or someone was watching out for her, because she found herself at a familiar brownstone building on the Upper West Side. She trudged up the stoop and knocked on the door.

A few moments later, the door flew open. "Astrid?" Deedee exclaimed as she held her robe tighter around her. "What are you doing—oh my Lord, it's freezing out there! Come in now!" She pulled Astrid inside her home. "Did you walk all the way here? Astrid ... Astrid, are you okay?"

She stood there, not moving. "Deedee ..." As the warmth began to seep back into her body, it was as if her brain had unfrozen too. "Oh, Dee," she cried before collapsing in her best friend's arms.

CHAPTER EIGHTEEN

"I just got off the phone with your mother," Deedee said as she entered the kitchen.

"And you didn't tell her the truth, right?" Astrid asked. "You made a pinky promise not to tell her."

"Of course not." She sat on the barstool next to her. "Pinky promises are 100 percent valid, no matter how old you are."

"Do you think she suspected anything?"

"I don't think so. I told her I had asked you to drive me to a conference I had to attend and that we had made the arrangements even before the Alpha punished you."

"Thank you. For everything."

"Anytime, Astrid." Deedee frowned. "So, what are you planning to do now?"

"Well," she began. "First I'm planning to eat this delicious chicken." She pointed to the whole roasted bird currently sitting on a serving plate in front of her. "Then

I'm going to work on those potatoes and the cornbread. After that, there's the pumpkin pie—hey! Give that back!"

Deedee had taken the plate and held it high over her head. "I'm not talking about food, you ninny."

"What's more important than food? I'm starving," she whined.

"We just demolished seven boxes of Chinese takeout while we watched a bunch of scary movies." Deedee put the plate down, but slid it away from Astrid. "You can't possibly still be hungry."

"Yes, I am." She reached for the potatoes instead.

"Astrid, please. I can only lie to your mother for so long." She placed an arm around her. "Talk to me."

"I've told you everything. That—that— he—" She stuffed her mouth full of mashed potatoes and swallowed. When she arrived here last night, it all came pouring out of her and she confessed everything to Deedee. About Zac. And what he said about Daric. Even thinking about it now hurt. Eating seemed to be the only thing right now that could help distract her. It was a good thing her stomach had turned into some kind of bottomless pit lately and she could pretty much shove food in her mouth every few hours.

"Yes, I know," Deedee said in a quiet voice. "And it's still hard to believe that ... about your dad. I can't believe it."

Neither did she, but here she was. Hiding out at her best friend's house while her entire world collapsed. It all turned out just as she predicted, but she'd allowed it to happen anyway. At first, she thought that maybe, just maybe, Zac would *at least* fight for them. But it sounded like he didn't even try. And if she were honest with herself, that was what hurt the most.

She still couldn't believe it about her father. Surely, Nick was lying. No, her father wasn't evil. He would never try to do anything to Cady or anyone else. "I don't want to talk about this anymore." The sound of her spoon hitting the bottom of the bowl of mashed potatoes made her cringe. "What's been going on with you and Cross?"

That question made Deedee's eyes bulge. "Nothing," she croaked.

"He's back in town, right?"

She shrugged. "Kind of. He's still busy and stuff and—"

"You just need to get off your ass and *tell him*."

Deedee raised a brow at her.

"Oh, boo. Don't look at me like that. Just because my love life's a disaster doesn't mean yours has to be."

"So, are you admitting that you love him?"

The question had her reaching for the cornbread. Hopefully this would keep her mouth busy and prevent her from answering that particular question. Did she love him? If she did, then she only had one thing to say about that: Love sucked. Big time.

"I came as soon as I could, *skatten min*."

The sound of her father's voice startled her more than his sudden appearance in front of Deedee's breakfast bar. "D-dad?" Bits of cornbread flew from her mouth and she reached for a glass of water to clear her air passage. "What are you—" She turned to Deedee. "You pinky promised," she accused.

"I pinky promised not to tell you mother," Deedee said. "But not your dad."

"Traitor," she mumbled.

"I'll give you guys some privacy." Deedee turned and walked out of the kitchen.

Daric gave her a nod and then walked around to Astrid's side.

"What did Deedee tell you?" she asked in a quiet voice.

"Enough." He placed an arm around her and pressed his lips to her forehead. "I'm sorry."

"For what?"

"For everything. For not being truthful. And that my past actions have caused you pain."

Her heart dropped all the way to her stomach. "So it's true. What Nick said about you. That you—"

"Yes. I used to work for Stefan, our enemy."

"But ... why ... I don't understand."

He let out a deep sigh and sat down on a stool next to her. "Stefan came to our village when I was a boy. He killed my father, your grandfather Jonas, so he could gain his powers. Then, he took my mother captive and forced me to do his bidding."

She gasped and then reached out to cover his hand with hers. "That's terrible, Dad. I'm so sorry."

"It was ... a gruesome time for me. I would have done anything to keep my mother alive."

"Including ... kidnapping Cady?"

He swallowed audibly. "He made me do a lot of horrendous things and to this day I have never quite forgiven myself, even though I did it to stop Stefan from hurting Signe. Kidnapping Cady seemed inconsequential then, just one of the many things I had to do to survive and keep my mother's life safe. Had I known how much it would have hurt you so, I would never have done it."

"But you didn't ... do anything else. I know you couldn't do that."

He shook his head. "No, I did not. Nick Vrost and the Lycans were able to save her before Stefan's plan came to fruition. And for that, I'm glad."

"What happened after, Dad?" she asked.

"Well, there's much more to the story, but basically, I met your mother, and she changed my life." His mouth curled up into a fond smile. "She was the light I needed in my life, to take away the darkness that had consumed me. Love changed me. It changed all of us. When all was said and done, we all decided it was best to keep my involvement with Stefan a secret. We all thought it was better to forget the past. Now I realize how wrong we were. Forgive me."

Despite the fact that she thought she'd cried every last tear she had the night before, she wiped at the tears that were pooling in the corner of her eyes. "It's okay. Thank you for telling me now." Strong arms enveloped her in a tight hug.

"Zac will come to his senses."

She stiffened. "Deedee told you—"

"I ... guessed." Daric pulled away and then wiped the tears that had tracked down her cheeks. "Do not be embarrassed, Astrid."

"I'm ... I'm not," she denied. "I'm just ... what you said about him coming to his senses ... even if he did, I don't really give a shit." The anger she had been feeling since yesterday had embedded itself deep in her chest. She held on to it, because right now, it was the only thing stopping her from feeling the pain he had caused.

"He does not know the whole story," Daric said. "He knows only one side."

"And he chose to believe his dad before learning our side."

"I'm not talking about our side."

Her father was being cryptic again. She shrugged. "It doesn't matter. Zac's made his position clear on this. It's over and done."

"If I could change the past, I would," Daric said. "But I cannot. Nick Vrost is not a bad man. He's loyal and solid as a rock, but just as unyielding. You will understand what it is like when it comes to your T—" He cleared his throat. "I mean, when you have your own family."

The thought of getting married and having children was the farthest thing from her mind right now. She never dared let herself fantasize about such things, not even when she was with Zac. It was probably because her brain was telling her she was making a mistake in getting involved with him. "What will you tell Mom?" she asked, hoping to change the subject.

"Your story is yours to tell," he replied. "But you cannot hide from her forever."

"I know."

"And you have duties to the clan and to the Alpha."

She cringed. "I'll come back to training tomorrow, I promise." Hopefully, Zac wouldn't show up at the training ever again. She would just have to endure Nick's disapproving glares, at least until the year was up and she was free.

"I'm afraid I'm not just talking about punishment," he said.

"What do you mean?"

"Grant and Frankie have decided that Lucas and Adrianna must ascend to Alpha status sooner rather than later. The ceremony is set to happen the day after tomorrow and will begin with a ball at the Waldorf Astoria."

"Oh, no." Placing her hands over the counter, she buried her face and let out a groan. "No. I can't."

"Attendance is mandatory."

"*Grrrr* ... can't you tell them I have the pox or something?"

Gently, he lifted her chin up with his finger. "Astrid, you need to come. I will be there; your mother and your brothers will be there."

And so will Zac. If he was going to become Beta, then of course he'd be there. "I don't have anything to wear."

"Yes you do," Dee piped in as she poked her head

through the kitchen doorway. "Sorry ... I couldn't help but overhear. But, remember you asked me to get rid of that dress? The one you wore to the wedding?"

"And I supposed you didn't?"

"It was a gorgeous dress, Astrid. I couldn't bear to throw it away. And you know you have to go."

"You cannot miss it, Astrid," Daric added. "It would be an insult to Lucas and Adrianna, and the entire clan."

Astrid sighed. "I'll make an appearance."

"I'll be your date," Deedee said cheerfully. "I just found out from my mother as well. We can make a fun night out of it."

She glanced at her father, who gave her a small smile. "All right. I'll stay for the ceremony and then I'm leaving." New York and New Jersey were the biggest Lycan clans in the world, plus there would be important people flying in from all over the world for the ball. Surely, she could avoid one person in a ballroom filled with hundreds of people.

CHAPTER NINETEEN

"Y**ou know, you really would look more handsome if you smiled.**"

Zac turned around and came face-to-face with Adrianna. The Lupa-to-be looked resplendent in a blue-green gown that matched both her eye colors. "I could say the same for you. This is your ascension ball, not a funeral."

Her expression faltered. "Yeah, yeah. I know."

"Is Jersey really that bad?" he asked.

She raised a thick, dark brow. "Have you lived there?"

He laughed. "No, but you would think it was the worst place in the world."

She sighed. "I don't know why the Lycan Council didn't just let my mother and father consolidate the territory into one. It would have been simpler for everyone."

Zac was still unsure why Adrianna was reluctant to take on the role of Lupa. It was her legacy, and her right.

She would be one of the few female Alphas in the world. A Lupa in her own right, not just the wife of an Alpha. "I'm sure it will be fine."

"I know. But, let's get back to you," she said. "What's got you tied up in knots? Still not sure about accepting the position at Fenrir and the role of Beta?"

Right about now, he wished that was his problem. Deciding on that would have been easier than what had really been torturing him the past few days. The sight of Astrid standing in the rain would be something he would never forget in his life.

You said I was yours.

His wolf growled at him. It had been furious the past two days, ripping him up from the inside. It wouldn't let him rest, displeased at what he had done. If only he could explain. If only it would understand. But it was an animal, and it wanted what it wanted. And it wanted Astrid.

It's better this way, he told himself. Blood and family were the most important thing in the world. He kept thinking of his mother's face. How disappointed she would be. Or how awful it would be for her to find out that he'd been sneaking around with the daughter of the man who—

"Zac?" Adrianna's face was now drawn into a look of concern. "Zac, I'm being serious now. What's the matter?"

"I'm fine, Adrianna." He leaned down and gave her a kiss on the cheek. "Enjoy your party."

He didn't want to walk away from his friend, but he was not in the mood to talk. Or even think. Maybe he could find some sort of distraction; drown himself in alcohol until he couldn't think straight. Or some other way to get his mind off Astrid. This was New York, after all, and there were lots of beautiful women out there, surely he could find one to help him forget Astrid. But the thought of even being with another woman made his stomach churn.

As he began to walk toward the doors, a hand looped around his arm, stopping him from going further. "Zac, where are you going?"

His mother's gentle voice shook him out of his thoughts. *This is for her,* he told himself. *You're doing this for her. The woman who gave you life.* "Mom," he greeted and kissed her on the temple. "You've done a marvelous job."

Despite the time constraints, The Grand Ballroom at the Waldorf Astoria looked absolutely stunning. The room was dressed up to the nines with flowers, huge crystal centerpieces on every table, and green and gold decor pieces all over. It must have taken an enormous effort and amount of time to pull this off, and only Cady Vrost would have been able to do it.

"I had a lot of help," she laughed. "But I am glad we were able to organize it all And that almost everyone could make it."

"This is a momentous occasion," he said. "I'm sorry, Mom, did you need me for anything? Otherwise, I did want to just pop out for some fresh air."

"Your Aunt Lara was looking for you. It's been ages since she's seen you and she wanted to say hello. Everyone from San Francisco's here, of course, including all your cousins."

Zac put on a tight smile. "Let's go and say hi then."

He allowed Cady to lead him back to the middle of the room where two women were standing by a cocktail table. They both looked similar though one was older, but not by much, at least, not at first glance.

"Zac, there you are!" Lara Henney embraced him in a full hug. "It's been so long! I haven't seen you since before you left for London."

"You look great, Aunt Lara." The older woman was dressed in a beautiful red ball gown the same shade as her hair.

"Hey, Zac," his cousin, Elise, greeted in a shy voice. She was almost a carbon copy of her mother, except for the eyes which were a stunning electric blue color. Her dress was the same shade, but much more modest, including the long silky gloves that covered her arms. Zac embraced her too, though she stiffened slightly at the contact.

"It's been a while, Elise. Why don't you ever visit us in New York? You guys used to do it all the time when you were younger."

She shrugged. "I just prefer to be at home."

"I had to drag her out here," Lara said. "And since my mother couldn't make it to the ball, we'll be visiting her upstate." Lara's mother, Vivianne, was the head of the New York coven. "Won't you come with us?"

"I'll try, Aunt Lara," he said. "So, where's Uncle Liam? Who else came with you?"

"Your Uncle Liam's around somewhere. Donovan's here too," she replied, referring to her eldest son. "Hmmm ... I thought I saw him ... oh, there he is." She narrowed her eyes toward the dance floor. "Who's that he's dancing with?"

Cady laughed. "Lara, don't you recognize her? That's Meredith and Daric's youngest. Astrid."

"Astrid?" Lara did a double take. "That's her? I always imagined her as that rebellious teen who shaved her head. *That* young woman is stunning."

The mention of her name made Zac freeze. Slowly, he turned to where his aunt was looking. Sure enough, dancing with his handsome cousin was Astrid. The sight of them made his mouth turn to dust.

Astrid indeed looked stunning. She was wearing a dress in varying shades of purple with a full skirt that flowed around her as she spun on the dance floor. A cape covered her shoulders, adding some modesty to the top, but when she twirled, he could see that the front plunged into a deep V. She threw her head back and laughed, and her long, lustrous hair shook around her like a golden waterfall.

A deep longing shot through him. And it was at that moment he knew he'd made a mistake. Seeing Astrid again, the way his heart just longed for her, made him realize that there could never be anyone else for him. It was time to stop living in the past. It was time to stop living the life others wanted for him.

"Excuse me," he said to his mother and cousin. He didn't even wait for them to acknowledge him before he started walking away. With each step he took, his feet felt like lead. He was dreading this, knowing there was a chance he could fail spectacularly and he would lose Astrid forever. *But I have to try. She has to know that—*

"Son, where are you going?"

Nick's chilly voice made him stop in his tracks. He didn't even turn around. "I'm going to her," he said. "I'm going to ask her to forgive me and take me back, even if I have to beg on my knees in front of everyone in this room."

"I warned you," his father hissed. "She's no good. She's—"

"Warned him about what?"

This time, they both froze. Cady stood behind them, her eyes narrowed and arms crossed over her chest. "What's going on? Nick? Zac? And don't say nothing, I'm not dumb!" Her eyes blazed with anger. "The two of you are so alike, I know when something's wrong. You two have been like fire kegs, waiting to explode."

Zac spoke first, gently wrapping his hands around her upper arms. "I'm sorry about what Daric did to you, but I have to do this. I can't live without her."

"What Daric—" Cady's expression instantly changed, and her eyes darted to Astrid and then to Nick. "Explain yourself, Nick. What did you tell our son about the past?"

Nick's jaw tightened. "The truth."

"But not the *whole* truth, I imagine." Cady turned to Zac. "Sweetheart, if you can't live without her, then *go after her*."

He stood there for a moment, stunned. "I ... thank you,

Mom." He gave her a quick hug and then picked up his pace as he made a beeline for Astrid.

The song had just ended, and Astrid and Donovan broke apart. "It's been great catching—hey, Zac, my man," his cousin greeted.

"Hello, Donovan."

"Dude, it's been too long." Donovan hugged him, but Zac remained stiff. "You never call or even visit. By the way, look who I bumped into. Astrid Jonasson." He gestured toward Astrid. "I can still remember when she would swim naked in my pool."

Zac felt the heat of combined anger and jealousy rage through him. His gaze zeroed in on Astrid, who had turned bright red.

"I was four years old the last time I did that," she said defensively.

Donovan chuckled. "I'm just kidding, Astrid. Besides, you're all grown up now."

It was too bad that the San Francisco Lycans were patriarchal, otherwise, Elise would have inherited the Alpha title. Because Zac was pretty sure he'd cause a major incident if he punched a future Alpha's teeth out. As the next song began to play, he cleared his throat and took ahold of his emotions. "I was hoping to dance with Astrid."

"Of course, cuz." Donovan gave a gracious bow out. "Be my guest. But save another dance for me, Astrid."

"Donovan, no—"

But Zac quickly took ahold of Astrid and spun her around before she could call to Donovan who was already walking away from them to join his mother and sister. Astrid struggled in his arms, but he held her in place. "Astrid, stop," he said.

She turned her head away from him. "I didn't say I would dance with you."

"I didn't ask." She tried to get away from him again, but he tightened his grip around her waist. "You could *poof* out of here, but you're not even trying."

She blew out a breath. "That's because I don't want everyone to see my abilities."

"Or you don't want to get away from me."

There was a barely-contained rage in her eyes when she looked up at him. "What do you want, Zac? Did you come to accuse my family of more crimes against yours? Or to—"

"Stop. Astrid, please. I was wrong. Wrong for just leaving you like that."

It looked like her expression faltered for a second, but the hardness in her eyes came back, like storm clouds suddenly appearing in the sky. "It's too late, Zac."

"Don't say that, Astrid. It's never too late." He searched for something—a little tenderness in her eyes or a spark of defiance. "Because I won't give up on you. On us."

"You already did!" she hissed at him, finally breaking free of his arms. "You did when you left me standing in the freezing rain." Tears began to flow down her cheeks. "When you broke my—" She sobbed, her hand going to her mouth.

The people around them were staring now, and Zac

could feel their eyes on them. But he didn't care. "I'm sorry, Astrid. And if it takes me a thousand lifetimes, I'll never stop asking for your forgiveness. Because I love you, and I need you in my life."

She sucked in a breath. "Zac, I—"

He never heard what she said after his name. A loud explosion filled the room and the sound wave it caused was enough to deafen him. There was a second explosion, and this time the force of it pushed him forward. He stretched his arms out to protect Astrid, then they stumbled to the floor. He cried out as pain shot through his eardrums but didn't move. When the ringing in his ears faded, the sound of chaos was all around them.

"Zac!" Astrid said as he was getting to his feet. "What's happening?"

"I don't know." He turned around. People were running everywhere. Most of them were guests, dressed up in their formal attire. Looking over to one side of the room, he saw two gigantic holes in the wall, the edges still burning. Smoke was everywhere. There was more screaming as a group of people streamed into the once-whole walls of the beautiful ballroom.

"Who the hell are those people?"

He didn't know, but he had an idea. Sure enough, some of them wore the same robes as the attackers from Deedee's party. But it wasn't just them. There were also men wearing dark clothing and holding guns. His blood froze like ice. The mages were here.

"Get out of here!" Zac said to Astrid. "Run. Go somewhere safe."

"What? No!" She gripped his shoulders. "I'm not leaving without you."

"I have to find my parents."

"Mine are here too," she pointed out. "And—oh shit!"

The men with guns began to fire into the crowd, dispersing them and had them stampeding toward the exits. Meanwhile, two large groups of mages had split up.

Zac had an idea where they would be going. Lucas and Adrianna. Already, he could hear the sounds of growling and clothes ripping as the Lycans began to shift, ready to fight their mortal enemies. But the mages weren't unprepared. He saw two wolves corner a mage. He laughed and threw something at them—a potion—and burst into a cloud of smoke. The wolves whimpered and cried out as they fell to the floor.

"No! Mom! Uncle Killian!" Astrid cried as she *poofed* away. She reappeared right by the fallen wolves.

"Astrid! Come back!" *Shit.* He had to get her away from here, somewhere safe. He called on his wolf, shifting into his animal form as soon as he could, ignoring the pain as his body reshaped itself. He was half-running, trying to get to Astrid. As he sprang across the room, he slowed down when he saw two mages standing over a prone and unconscious Adrianna. *Fuck.* He couldn't let them get to her, but Astrid—

A large, gray wolf leapt from out of nowhere and knocked both mages down. It raised its gigantic head and briefly, their eyes met. The wolf's eyes were a rich cobalt blue. He didn't know anyone from the New York clan with such a distinct eye color or that color fur. It was really more silver than gray. Its maw opened wide, baring its teeth as it bore down on one of the mages' head, while a large paw swiped at the other.

Zac sighed with relief inwardly. Adrianna was saved by the wolf, whoever it was. He pushed his wolf's body forward, making it all the way across the room to stop in front of Astrid as she cradled the white wolf in her arms.

"Mom ... Mom ..." she cried. "No ..."

"She'll be all right, I'll take care of her." Daric said as he materialized beside Astrid. He picked up his mate and then turned to Zac. "The mages are banking on the chaos. You must not let them get to Lucas."

Zac nodded and turned tail. Astrid would be safe with her father. *He'll bring her to safety.* For now, he had to find Lucas and make sure the mages did't take him.

The entire room was in pandemonium. He guessed that was the plan—to cause as much panic and destruction as possible so the Lycans wouldn't know what hit them. But he kept his focus, filtering out all the distractions around him until he found—

Lucas!

Two men in black held his arms as he was on his knees. His head hung limply, though he still struggled. *Drugged,* Zac thought. A man in a red robe stood in front of him.

"You thought you had gotten rid of us!" the man hissed. "But you have merely slowed us down. A new

Magus has come forth!" He held up his hand and some-thing began to glow in his hand. No, it wasn't glowing. It was on fire. The fireball grew larger and larger as he extended his palms. "When I make this sacrifice and take the blood power from this creature, I will be the most powerful Master Mage the world has ever seen!" He raised his arms high and aimed his sights on Lucas.

He ran as fast as he could, his hind legs giving one last push as he leapt forward. One of the mages holding Lucas down saw him and let out a shout. But it was too late. The man in the red robe released the fireball.

Zac tumbled in front of Lucas and he waited for the heat and flames. But it never came. When he got to his feet he saw why.

No!

His heart ripped into two when he saw the figure engulfed in flames. The long hair, the billowy skirt, and the cape. Astrid had put herself between Lucas and the flames, to save him and stop the mages.

He wasn't sure what happened next. It was like he was watching a movie play in front of his eyes as his wolf took over. His animal hurtled toward the man in the red robe. He must not have expected it as the man's red eyes grew wide with fright. The wolf landed on top, pinning him to the ground as the animal went straight for his throat.

The man didn't even have time to scream as Zac's wolf ripped out his vocal chords. Warm blood gushed into its mouth, flowing down its jaws. The rage and grief wouldn't let it stop, as it kept chomping down on the man's neck and shoulders.

"Zachary, stop! Stop!" came a familiar voice.

He felt himself being lifted away by an invisible force. The wolf continued to struggle, not quite done with its revenge, despite the fact that the man was already dead and half his body practically decimated.

"No!" he half-growled and half-snarled as his human side ripped out of his wolf's body. He got to his feet. The anger and fury inside him wouldn't let him stop. He would kill every last one of these mages for what they did to Astrid.

"Zachary, calm down," Daric said as he appeared in front of Zac. He wrapped an arm around his shoulder to pull him back.

"Calm down! What the fuck, Daric! They killed her! Your daughter! My ..." He broke down, the anguish and pain replacing his anger. "Astrid."

"Zachary, open your eyes." His voice was oddly calm. "Open your eyes so you can see what's right in front of you."

"Open my eyes?" Maybe Daric had gone mad with grief too. "What do you mean?"

Daric stared back at him with those strange, blue-green eyes. "There."

He looked toward where Astrid's body had burned right before him. He blinked several times, as he wasn't sure what he was seeing.

Aunt Lara was kneeling down, her arms around a

woman who was completely naked, her face obscured by her blonde hair. Lara had found a length of fabric—probably a table cloth—to wrap around the young woman. When the young woman lifted her head, their eyes locked.

His heart leapt out of his chest. "No, it couldn't—" But he was already running toward her, unable to control his feet. "Astrid!"

She looked up at him, her eyes wide with fright. "Zac! I don't understand ... I saw that fireball about to hit you and I just ... it was hot but I wasn't burning."

"You're alive." He slipped his hands under her arms and pulled her to him, inhaling that achingly familiar scent. "You're alive. I thought you'd died."

"Astrid, darling," Lara said. "Did you ... I mean, you leapt in front of the fireball, but you weren't burned up?"

She shook her head. "No, Aunt Lara. I mean, I could have sworn I did. But maybe it wasn't a real fireball?"

"Your clothes were all singed away," she said. "But you're unharmed?"

"I guess?" Astrid looked down at her arms. "Nothing. Not a scratch."

Lara's gaze darted from Zac to Astrid. "Uh, I might have a theory."

"What is it?" Zac asked. "What do you know, Aunt Lara?"

"Er," the older woman hesitated. "Astrid, darling, is there even a small chance you could be ... pregnant?"

"*Pregnant?*" both Zac and Astrid said at the same time.

"Zac, Astrid," Daric called as he approached them.

"What your Aunt Lara is trying to say is that if Astrid is pregnant with her True Mate's child, it may explain why she didn't burn in the fire. She's indestructible."

Zac allowed the information to sink in. Pregnant. Astrid was pregnant. And it was his. He had no doubt. "Astrid ..."

Her face had gone ashen. "I can't ... it's not ..." She turned to her father. "Dad, did you know?"

Daric went silent.

"Astrid," Zac began. "Talk to me. Please."

"I need ... some ..." She tried to stand up, but her legs seemed wobbly, so Zac caught her. "It doesn't make sense ... you and me, True Mates?"

Zac pulled her into an embrace. "It makes perfect sense to me, sweetheart. I told you, I love you."

"The mages," she said suddenly. "And Mom!"

"Your mother is fine," Daric said. "I took her to the Lycan medical facility in The Enclave. And our enemies have been subdued by the Lycan Security Team. We were prepared for them to attack us, but I must admit, we were surprised that they would bring humans with them or that they would be so bold as to stage a head-on attack."

Lara's face went pale. "Were the humans under the control of the mages?"

Daric's face darkened. "It didn't seem like it."

"Can I see Mom?" Astrid said.

"She's still recovering for now. But I will take you to her, when you are ready."

"For now," Lara said. "We'll leave you two to talk. Daric?"

The warlock nodded. "I shall be helping with the cleanup. Call me when you are ready to leave."

"I will." She hugged her father.

"Astrid," Zac began. "Are you really all right?"

"I can't explain it … but I am. I—"

He embraced her tight, inhaling her scent and reveling in the feeling that she was here. Alive. "I'm so sorry, Astrid. For everything. Please. Forgive me." He got down on his knees pressed his cheek against her stomach, and then realization dawned that their child was in there. A new life, one that was half of them both. "I know I don't deserve you. I acted like an idiot, and I should have fought harder for us.

She took a deep breath. "I was so angry at you, that you just left like that. But I know that you were thinking of your mother. What happened to her was horrible, and my dad has had to live with what he did every day. But we can't keep paying for the mistakes of our parents or living in the past." She cupped his chin in her hands and tilted his face up. "I don't know what came over me. I was watching that man, and he was going to hurt you and I just … *poofed*. I was halfway across the room and I didn't even think about it. I just appeared where I wanted to be. Because I couldn't let you die."

She was crying now, and he got up so he could wipe the tears from her cheeks. "You couldn't?"

"No. Not without telling you that I love you, too."

Zac thought he was dreaming. Or that he had died. "Astrid ... I love you so much." He held her beautiful face in his hands and leaned down to claim her lips in a passionate kiss. God, she was the sweetest thing he'd ever tasted. For days he thought he would never get to hold her in his arms again, and now here she was. "If you forgive me, I promise you I'll never let you go."

She looked up at him, her eyes shining with love. "Just kiss me again, and I'll forgive everything."

CHAPTER TWENTY

The cleanup at the Waldorf Astoria took hours. As Daric had explained, the Lycan Security Team had been prepared for an attack, but even though they had run through every scenario, they didn't expect such a direct assault or counted on any human allies.

They all decided to regroup at The Enclave, in Grant and Frankie's penthouse, as they were at least sure the magical protections there were still strong. Once again, most of the New York Lycans, plus their allies from San Francisco, were there. They all knew the situation was serious, so even though it was the wee hours of the morning, they all managed to drag themselves there for the debriefing.

Astrid sat in one of the loveseats with Zac beside her, his arm around her shoulders. Nick and Cady were the last to enter and she felt Zac stiffen. She reached over and covered his hand with hers.

"... the good news is that there were no casualties on our side," Grant said as he continued his assessment of the situation. "The bad news is that the mages are back, in bigger numbers, and it seems that they've recruited human allies."

"They've been hiding their presence from us," Daric continued. "And as we have figured out, they are trying to stop the next generation of Alphas from ascending."

"That mage said the only way he could become a master mage was by taking my 'blood's power'," Lucas said. "What did he mean?"

"Lucas and Adrianna, as the children of two Alphas, are more powerful than any of us know," Cross said. "It's not like us hybrids, but they are unique."

"Lycans used to have the ability to use magic," Daric said. "And maybe it's coming back."

"How?" Adrianna asked. "We don't have any witch or warlock blood in us."

"Love is a kind of magic," Daric said. "And because you are children of two Alphas, born of a True Mate pairing, your blood is more powerful than you think."

"In any case," Grant said. "You both will ascend to Alpha as soon as we can arrange for the ceremony."

"Adrianna." Frankie turned to her daughter. "You need to move to New Jersey as soon as possible. Consolidate your power and take control of your territory."

"Consolidate my power?" she asked. "What do you mean?"

Her mother sighed. "The Jersey Clan has grown so much over the past decades, especially with the open border policy your father and I had when we were married. But aside from that, I'm afraid that I've been remiss in my duties and have allowed certain forces to run wild, but no more. Not when there's so much at stake."

"Lucas, you also need to choose your Beta," Grant said. "Someone who can be by your side and watch your back. Someone who will protect this clan along with you and help you make the right decisions."

"I'm happy to serve as long as you need me," Nick said. "But you may want someone who could give you a fresh perspective on things. And younger and stronger, of course, who can keep up with you."

"I've thought long and hard about this," Lucas said. "I wanted someone not only loyal to me and the clan, but who could also be strong enough to stand up to me if I'm not making the right decisions. And needless to say, a person who would sacrifice their life for the clan. And so, I choose Astrid Jonasson."

"What the fuck?" Astrid would have shot to her feet, if Zac wasn't holding her hand. "M-m-me? Beta?"

"Yes, you." Lucas said. "Astrid, twice you've saved my life. Yes, tonight you literally put yourself between me and a fireball, but also the other night at Blood Moon, you were strong enough to knock me down, even though I was in bloodlust. I need someone who won't be afraid of me ... or to take me on if needed."

"I ... I don't know what to say." Her mind was reeling. She looked over at Zac. At first, she thought he would protest, not wanting her to be in harm's way, but his face was shining with pride. "Zac? I though you would want—"

"Sweetheart." He took her hand in his. "I would prefer you to be safe at home, raising our children and never having to deal with all this ugliness. But you and I know that you wouldn't be satisfied with that. You trained for this. Were born for this. And whatever you decide, I will support you."

"I don't know ... this is all too fast."

"Nothing's set in stone," Lucas said. "But I do hope you consider it."

"Well, I wasn't expecting that," Grant said, then he let out a deep breath. "But of course, as Alpha, you have the right to choose, Lucas." He turned to everyone else. "We have already begun our preparations to defend ourselves from future attacks."

"And not just defend ourselves," Frankie said. "This time, we are going to actively seek out the mages and put a stop to them once and for all."

"Tomorrow, we'll start outlining our plans. Anyone is welcome to join us in this fight, but I totally understand if you are reluctant."

"You know we're behind you," Liam Henney, Alpha of the San Francisco clan, said.

"All of us," Sebastian Creed added. "You'll have all my resources at your disposal."

"Good. We're setting up a command center at a secret location and we will give you more details." Grant rubbed his temple. "I have more cleanup to do, so those of you who want to rest, can go home."

Astrid was still shocked, and it took a gentle nudge from Zac to make her stand up. Daric and Meredith, who had recovered fully, came up to congratulate her.

"My baby's going to be Beta! Can you believe it?" Meredith said.

"Mom!" Astrid said. "I haven't said yes, yet. Lucas," she began. "Are you absolutely sure?"

"I am," Lucas said, his mismatched eyes serious. "I know you'll do a good job."

"What about Zac?" she asked. "Shouldn't he be in line next?"

Zac laughed. "Oh no, not me," he said. "Even if Lucas asked me, I would have said no."

"Why not?" Astrid asked, then her heart sank. "Are you going back to London?"

"What? No way." He slipped a hand around her waist, his hand cupping over her belly. "I'm not leaving you. I'm moving back to New York. Except—"

"Zac."

Astrid winced at the sound of Nick Vrost's voice. Beside her, Zac flinched, but turned around to face his father. Nick stood there, with Cady by his side. "May I have a word, son?"

"Dad," he said in a terse voice. His grip around Astrid tightened. "If you say anything to upset *my mate*, I won't be responsible for what I do or say."

Astrid shivered at the deadly seriousness of Zac's voice.

"I've only come here to ask for her forgiveness."

Both Astrid and Zac were stunned into silence. "Forgiveness?" Astrid managed to croak.

Nick looked down at Cady, who smiled at him and squeezed his hand. "Your mother reminded me about something. About how, a long time ago, a very stubborn old man with prejudices of his own almost caused me to ruin my own life and leave my mate. And how that same, stubborn old man somehow swallowed his pride enough to ask for forgiveness when he realized he was in the wrong. I always wondered what made Vasili change his mind about your mother, and now I know. Family is the most important thing in the world."

The tension from Zac's shoulders seemed to drain away. "What do you mean exactly?"

"Astrid," he began. "I'm sorry. Sorry that I made Zac hurt you. I told him the truth, but not the whole truth. Yes, Daric was involved with the mages and kidnapped Cady, but he also saved Zac's life."

"Right before the Battle of Norway, Stefan kidnapped you," Cady continued, her voice shaking. "He ripped you right from my arms. Daric was the one who saved you. We didn't tell you all of this because we thought that the past is past. We wanted to put it all behind us."

"But, perhaps, we shouldn't forget." Nick said. "Forgetting the past is what allowed the mages to come into power again."

"This is all so confusing," Astrid said.

"I know, and I'm sorry. We all are." Nick's voice turned somber. "I asked your father for his forgiveness long ago. Cady forgave me too, so quickly that I'm still boggled by it. But ... I think I have yet to forgive myself for failing to keep them safe and save them in the first place."

"Nick," Cady began. "You didn't fail us. We're here now. All of us are here because you've always protected this clan."

Nick turned back to Astrid. "You don't have to forgive me now. And I would be honored if you allowed me to help you transition into your new role as Beta, should you accept it."

"I ... of course," she said. "And ... yes, I forgive you, Nick." She turned to Cady. "Thank you."

"Don't thank me," Cady said. "Well, I did kind of knock some sense into my stubborn husband, but he realized most of it all on his own."

"And that, son," Nick said to Zac. "Is why we need our True Mates. To keep us on the straight and narrow. And to help us believe in ourselves when we're in doubt."

"Oh my God!" Cady exclaimed. "I almost forgot. Astrid ... Zac ... Oh ..." She launched herself forward and embraced them both. "You both ... I'm going to be a grandmother! Nick! We're going to be grandparents." She was crying now, tears of joy pouring down her face.

"Wait, what am I missing?" Meredith cried. "What's going on?"

Astrid had forgotten that her mother had been in the medical wing for the last couple of hours. "Er, well, Mom, so it turns out Zac and I are True Mates."

"What?" Meredith said. "I thought you guys were just boinking."

Astrid went red. "What do you mean? You knew all this time?"

"I'm your mother, Astrid," Meredith said. "I know everything. And you'll know everything about your kids too when—" And then the realization soon hit her. "*Motherfucking truck nuts*! I'm going to be a grandmother!" She hopped over to Cady and hugged her. "We're going to be grandmas!"

Cady just laughed and hugged her in return. "Yes, we are."

"Can I get the cool grandma name?" Meredith said. "I like Lulu or Gigi. You can be Grams."

"Whatever you want, Meredith," Cady said, her face beaming. She looked up at Daric. "I'm honored to be sharing a grandchild with the people who saved my son."

"Well, *old man*," Grant teased as he came up beside Nick. "Ready to be a grandpa?"

"You might not be far behind," Nick said. "You know these True Mates pairing seems to happen in clusters."

Grant chuckled. "I can only imagine. I only hope my grandchildren's arrivals won't be quite as dramatic."

It seemed everyone there had gathered and were now

crowding around them to offer their congratulations and well wishes.

"A ray of hope and happiness for now," Aunt Lara said. "Something to look forward to, since we may be facing dark times ahead."

"But, haven't we proven that we will always win?" Frankie said. "The mages may be powerful and have magic, but there's something we have they never will."

"We have family," Daric finished. "And we have love. That's something Stefan never understood and ultimately, what led to his defeat."

"And we'll win again," Lucas said, his face drawn into steely determination. "I'll do my damned best to make sure it happens.

Zac looked at his friend. "We all will."

And Astrid knew that she too, would be doing her part to keep them all safe. She already knew what her answer to Lucas' offer would be. But for now, surrounded by the most important people in the world to her, she would bask in the glow of their love.

———

Grant had offered to take out the champagne to celebrate, but everyone was just too exhausted. Besides, Astrid realized that being pregnant, she couldn't stand the thought of alcohol anyway. And so, they all retired, and Zac and Astrid went back to his hotel suite, declining his parents' offer to stay in Zac's old room.

"What, you never snuck in girls there?" Astrid had teased as they left The Enclave.

"No."

She snorted. "Of course not. You were the golden boy, Goody Two-shoes, weren't you?"

"I'll show you how much of a Goody Two-shoes I am."

And so he did, multiple times that night, until she once again begged for him to let her sleep. In the morning, she didn't even want to wake up and get out of bed. This whole making a human thing was making her tired.

"Astrid, come into the living room," Zac called. "I have something to show you."

"Ugh! No," she protested. "I'm not falling for that one again!"

"I have breakfast," he said.

Her stomach gurgled loudly and she rolled out of the bed. Apparently, that was another symptom of being pregnant with a True Mate's pup—increased appetite. Her mother joked that she had nearly eaten them out of house and home for each of her pregnancies.

She reached for Zac's discarded shirt on the floor and slipped it on. "I swear to God, Zachary Vrost, if you're standing out there with your dick in your hand, I'm going to—" She sucked in a breath. "That's not your dick."

He laughed. "No, it's not." Zac was down on one knee, a small velvet box in his palm. When he opened it, she gasped. A huge diamond ring stared up at her.

"Zac ... how did you ..."

"This ring belonged to my great-grandmother," he said.

"My mother was keeping it safe for me. I asked her to bring it here this morning. So, Astrid, will you do me the honor of being my wife?"

She let out a squeal. "Duh! Of course!"

Zac promptly put the ring on her finger and then stood up. "I love you, Astrid."

"I love you too, you crazy man," she laughed in between his kisses.

"Crazy?"

"Well, what kind of man would be in love with me? A loony one, I tell you. Hey!" She shrieked in protest as he lifted her up in his arms and brought her back to bed.

"I'll show you how crazy I am," he said, as he pushed her down on the mattress.

Their lovemaking that morning was wild and urgent. Last night, Zac had taken his time, as if savoring her and making it last as long as possible. This morning was different, but no less tender or sweet.

"So," she began, as she looked at the hunk of rock on her finger. They were cuddled up together, Zac behind her, kissing her neck. "What are you going to do now? Are you going to take Lucas' position at Fenrir?"

"I was about to tell you last night," he said. "But we were interrupted. Anyway, I plan to quit."

"Quit?" she asked.

"Yeah, now that my fiancée is going to be Beta of the most powerful Lycan clan, she can bring home the bacon —Ow!" She had slapped him on the arm.

"You're kidding, right?" she said, twisting around to

face him. "I mean, I'm happy with whatever you want to do but, quitting doesn't seem like you."

He kissed her on the nose. "Yes, I'm kidding. I mean, not about the quitting part. But there's something I've always thought of doing."

"And what is that?"

"Well, Vasili always hoped that my father would take over the family holdings. He's got companies and properties in Europe and all over the world. But all my dad wanted to do was work for Fenrir and be Beta. So, when he died, everything went into a trust."

"I see."

"And so, I was thinking, Vasili always wanted a Vrost to run everything, so why not me? I'm going to talk to my father about it as soon as I can."

"Oh, Zac, that's a wonderful idea," she said. "I can't think why you wouldn't make it successful."

"It's scary, but ... I know this is what I want to do."

"I could always go back to The Vixen Den if you run all the businesses to the ground," she joked. "The girls there always said I could make a killing with my tits."

"Oh, ha ha," he shot back. "Maybe I should work at that male warlock strip club downtown."

"Uncle Merlin's place?" she said. "I don't know, they have very high standards. Hey!" She giggled as he rolled her over and tickled her. "Stop! Stop, Zac!"

"No more talk of strip clubs. Male or otherwise, okay?" he said.

"I ... I ... no more!" She wiped the tears from her eyes.

"How about we talk weddings? What kind of wedding would you like?"

"Whatever you want, sweetheart," he said. "As long as you're there and our families are there."

"Well, of course! I can't wait to tell—" She slapped her hand on her forehead. "Shit! Deedee!"

He frowned at her. "What about Deedee?"

"I didn't see her last night at the Alpha's penthouse." She chewed on her lip. "We came together to the ball, but then Donovan came to ask me to dance—stop looking at me like that, Zachary, he's like a brother to me—and then I haven't seen her since."

"If Deedee was hurt, we would have known. Sebastian was at the meeting and he didn't seem distressed."

"True." She thought for a moment. "I should check on her."

"Of course, do you what you need to do."

After several phone calls, what seemed like a hundred text messages, and enough voice messages to fill her inbox, Astrid was starting to worry that something did happen to Deedee. When it was late afternoon and still no word, Zac drove her to Deedee's place.

"Dee?" she called as she rapped on the door when she wouldn't answer the doorbell. She let out a deep breath. "Okay, Deedee," she shouted. "I'm coming in!" She closed her eyes and visualized Deedee's living room. Somehow, she figured out that being pregnant with Zac's baby amplified her powers, so she was able to go more than six feet. Hopefully this would work. *Now or never.*

When the soft *poof* sound popped in her ears, she found herself in the middle of Deedee's living room.

"What the—Astrid?" Deedee cried.

"Deedee!" Astrid collapsed on the couch. "Where have you been? Where did you go? And why haven't you been answering my calls? And have you been crying?"

Deedee's pretty face was all blotchy and her eyes were swollen. Her nose was red and her cheeks were puffy. "I ... just need to be alone for a bit, okay?"

Astrid looked around her. There were tissues everywhere and the TV was blasting. "What are you watching? Oh my God, is that a documentary about serial killers?"

"I needed something to cheer me up."

"Cheer you ... oh no!" Astrid grabbed the remote and turned the TV off. "Deedee, talk to me. What happened?"

"Astrid," she sniffed. "I ... last night, I spoke to Cross."

"You did?"

She nodded then wiped her eyes with the back of her hand. "I thought we were going to die when the mages attacked. Then I saw you and Zac and realized what you guys were ... and so I went to Cross and confessed my feelings."

"What did he say?"

More tears poured down her cheeks. "I ... he ..." She let out a hiccup. "He said, 'I'm sorry, Dee. I love you, but only as a friend.'"

Astrid's heart dropped. "Oh, no. Dee. Dee! I'm so sorry." She wrapped her arms around her. "I'm so, so sorry." She wanted to cry too. Well, she wanted to kill

Cross first, and then cry. "This is my fault," she said. "I shouldn't have pushed you so hard."

"Astrid, this isn't your fault." She blew her nose into a fresh tissue. "I shouldn't have let my feelings grow so deep. It was good I found out now anyway."

"I just ... Deedee, you're my best friend," she began. "I don't have any sisters, and I just thought it would be so cool if you were my best friend and my real sister too."

"Astrid, you silly girl. You *are* my sister." She let out a resigned sigh and then took Astrid's hand. "The moment I saw you in your crib when I first came to visit, I knew it. I told your mom that I was going to be your big sister. You're my sister, Astrid, not by blood, but one that I choose."

"Stop, Deedee, you're really going to make me cry." She reached for a tissue. "Sorry, this must be what they say about pregnancy hormones."

"It's all right, Astrid." Deedee hugged her close. "And don't feel bad about what you have with Zac. It's one in a million finding someone like that. I'm so very glad for you both." She turned Astrid's hand over to look at the ring. "And congratulations."

"Thank you." She couldn't help but feel sad, despite Deedee's words. Her best friend's—no, her sister's—heart was broken into pieces and here she was, waving her giant engagement ring in her face. "Maybe Cross just needs time and—"

"No, Astrid," she said. "He was pretty clear last night. Believe me. Hey, it's all right. I promise, I won't let things get weird and I'll be your maid of honor."

"You will?"

"Of course!" She put on a bright smile. "I'll never forgive you if you choose anyone else."

"Never." Astrid squeezed her hand. "Sisters. Forever."

"Sisters," Deedee replied. "Now, when do we start the wedding planning?"

"Zac and I haven't made real plans, but we can wait. Oops." She had nearly forgotten about him waiting outside. "Actually, give me a minute. I need to call him to let him know he should go home.

"Go home ... Astrid, is he out there? Don't make your mate wait out there in cold," she said.

"He's got heated seats in his Porsche," she retorted. "He can wait a while longer."

They talked some more about wedding planning, but when Astrid started fussing over Dee, she declared she was tired of Astrid's mother hen routine. "You're worse than *my* mother," she said as she escorted Astrid to the door. "Go. Get out."

"Fine. But you call me, anytime, okay?"

"Yes, *Mom*."

After one final long hug, Astrid left and headed to where Zac was parked in front of Deedee's building.

"Everything okay?" he asked as he stepped out of the car. "Sweetheart, what's wrong?" She told him everything, and he pulled her into an embrace. "I'm sorry," he said, kissing her palm. "Dee's my friend, too. I don't want her to suffer like this."

She pressed her cheek against his wool coat, taking in

his yummy Christmassy scent. "I'm just so mad, you know. How could Cross do that to her?" she fumed. "He's just been acting so weird lately. I thought maybe that now he's back, he and Dee could live happily ever after too, and, you know, it's nice to be with the person you love."

"It is," he agreed, then leaned down to kiss her on the lips. "But, sweetheart, if he doesn't feel the same way, you can't force him to love her."

"I know. I just wish ..." She looked at Deedee's door. "I just hope she won't do anything drastic."

"Deedee's a smart, level-headed girl," he said. "She'll be fine. We'll look out for her. She's not just our friend. She's family."

"Thank you," she said. "For being here."

"Of course." He reached down to rub her stomach. "Let's go home. You must be hungry."

Her stomach gurgled on cue. "Starving," she laughed.

"We can't let our baby get hungry."

She leaned into him, enjoying the feeling of his arms around her, warming her up on this chilly winter morning. The street was unusually quiet for New York, so all she could hear was the sound of his breathing and his heart-beat. "Take me home, Zac."

"With pleasure."

EPILOGUE

Some might say pulling off an entire wedding in two weeks was impossible, but not for the combined forces of the New York Lycan clan and their allies. In that short time, they had a judge, caterers, flowers, a cake, a custom-made wedding dress, and all the trimmings of a grand affair all ready.

The bride and groom weren't fussy about the details, as long it ended with them married by the end of the day. However, there was one thing the bride wouldn't budge on: the venue. Their parents wanted the entire wedding to take place in The Enclave for safety reasons. But Astrid refused because she knew that she wouldn't be able to invite any non-Lycans or non-members of the clan to the wedding.

After much fighting, they relented, and with several protection spells cast by the groom's great-aunt and a solid security plan, they were able to have the wedding at a beautiful glass-covered rooftop garden in Brooklyn. While Deedee served as maid of honor, the three bridesmaids consisted of Astrid's closest friends from The Vixen Den. Petal, Fantasy, and Coco looked stunning in their custom-made bridesmaid dresses as they walked down the aisle. Mr. G, on the other hand, sat on the bride's side, looking thoroughly pleased with himself, perhaps satisfied with the thought that those two crazy kids wouldn't have gotten here without him.

The rest of the guests consisted of family, including all of the bride and groom's siblings, plus those they considered family, even if not by blood.

The ceremony wasn't too long, no need for pomp and fuss; after all, they knew that they were mates and that was all they needed. Plus, after the stress of the wedding, Astrid said she needed as much party time as possible, even if she couldn't have any alcohol.

The snow fell outside, but it was toasty warm inside the glass conservatory. Zac knew that the snow would always remind him of Astrid, of her wearing that ridiculous robe when they saw each other that night at The Vixen and the first time they made love in that cabin. It seemed fitting that they would be married under the snow, too.

He surveyed the space, impressed at how quickly it had been transformed from the ceremony to reception area. Round tables with stunning floral and crystal centerpieces replaced the rows of chairs and the aisle. Fairy lights twinkled overhead. A quartet played in the corner.

Elegantly-dressed waiters made sure the champagne was overflowing.

"You did a great job, Mom," he said as he approached Cady. He leaned down and kissed her on the cheek. "Not that I ever doubted you." Only the great Cady Vrost could pull off such a feat.

"It was a team effort," she assured her son.

"And you did a great job keeping the peace between the bride and the mother of the bride, too."

Cady chuckled. "Now *that*, I'd like to take credit for."

"Or an award." He shook his head. "Those two. They're so alike they can't even see it."

Astrid and Meredith had clashed over just about every detail of the wedding, and of course, he had to hear his fiancée complain nearly every day. He wondered if Daric had the patient of a saint or if he somehow had a secret magic spell that helped him cope with the two women in his life.

"Where is your bride, by the way?" Cady asked. "Oh, there she is."

Zac looked around. Astrid was in the middle of the dance floor, waltzing with her new father-in-law. She looked absolutely radiant as Nick spun her around, giggling as he twirled her a few more times than necessary.

"I think I'll go dance with my wife," he said. The word made a warm feeling buzz through him. Wife. Astrid was his *wife*.

"Yes, please," Cady said. "And make sure you send your father my way. He still owes me a dance."

He made his way through the crowd, gently nudging people aside as he was in a hurry to get to Astrid. "Excuse me." One particular gentleman didn't seem to want to budge from his spot. "*Excuse me*," he repeated.

The hulk of a man in his way turned around. Zac's wolf raised its hackles, sensing the other man's agitation. Or rather, his wolf's agitation. It felt like a tightly reined beast, wanting to get out. He also seemed familiar, but he was sure he would have remembered him if they had met before. For one thing, this man was built like a Mac truck, but also, his hair was pure silver, but his face was youthful; looked like he was only in his mid-thirties at the most. "Do I know you?"

Cobalt blue eyes stared back at him with a fiery glare. "No, you don't," he said before turning around and walking away.

Zac would have called one of the members of the security team, but the man headed straight for the stairwell exit. *Strange.* Maybe he was from Astrid's side, one of her Lycan cousins from West Virginia perhaps. Shaking the thoughts out of his head, he strode to his wife. He tapped his father on the shoulder.

"May I cut in?"

Nick's face broke into a smile. "Of course." He gave his son a clap on the arm. "I'll go look for your mother. She's probably annoyed that I haven't danced with her yet." He gave Astrid a kiss on the cheek before walking away.

Astrid's mouth curled into a sly smile. "Now I know where you get your dance moves from."

He took her hand, then placed his other palm on her waist. "I'll have you know, Garret said I was a much better dancing partner than my dad."

"Garret said—you're joking right?"

"Joking? My great-grandfather was serious about dancing. And Garret was a great practice partner," he said.

"Better than me?" she asked.

"Well, he was very graceful and—*Ow!*" That earned him a playful slap on the shoulder. "Well, I can tell you one thing. You look much better in that dress."

She smirked. "Flattery will get you everywhere, Mr. Vrost."

"I hope it does, Mrs. Vrost." He pulled her close and leaned down close to her ear. "I have to say though, this is my third favorite outfit you've ever worn."

"Third?" she asked. "This is a Hannah Taylor Muccino Bridal original. Hannah herself worked day and night to get it ready and it's not even your second favorite?"

"Well, my second favorite outfit is that robe you were wearing that night at The Vixen Den."

"That one?" She laughed. "Even my mother said I looked like a stripper. What's the first favorite outfit?"

"That dress you wore at the ball." He brushed his mouth lightly against the shell of her ear, which made her shiver. "That was the dress, right? If I had seen you wearing it at Hannah's wedding, I wouldn't have said no if you asked me to dance."

"You wouldn't have?"

"No. And I probably would have asked you first. Then taken you home and had my way with you."

She gasped when his licked at the spot behind her ear. "Would it be bad if we had a quickie in the bathroom?"

"Definitely," he replied, giving her a wicked smile. "And probably frowned upon. We can't leave until the guests have had their fun."

Her lips curled down into a pout. "Fine."

He gave her a quick kiss on the lips, twirled her, then pulled her back to his chest. "I love you, Astrid," he said in the slightest whisper.

Cradling his face in her soft palms, she stared up at him. "I love you, too."

There would be challenges ahead, not just for them, but for all of their loved ones. He knew he would fight hard and do his damnedest to make sure they would prevail over their enemies and protect Astrid, their pup, and the entire clan.

But for now, as they danced under the fairy lights and snow continued to whirl outside, he focused on his wife, holding her close and enjoying this moment.

The End

———

I hope you enjoyed Astrid and Zac's happy ever after.

I have some extra HOT bonus scenes for you - just join my newsletter here to get access:
http://aliciamontgomeryauthor.com/mailing-list/

You'll get access to ALL the bonus materials from all my books and my **FREE** novella **The Last Blackstone Dragon.**

ABOUT THE AUTHOR

Alicia Montgomery has always dreamed of becoming a romance novel writer. She started writing down her stories in now long-forgotten diaries and notebooks, never thinking that her dream would come true. After taking the well-worn path to a stable career, she is now plunging into the world of self-publishing.

f facebook.com/aliciamontgomeryauthor

🐦 twitter.com/amontromance

BB bookbub.com/authors/alicia-montgomery

Printed in the USA
CPSIA information can be obtained
at www.ICGtesting.com
LVHW090355151023
761121LV00001BA/211